ENGLISH ASSASSIN

A STIRLING HUNT MISSION

STEWART CLYDE

Published by Hunt Press in 2021.

Copyright © Stewart Clyde 2021.

The moral right of Stewart Clyde to be identified as the Author of the Work has been asserted by him, in accordance with the Copyrights, Designs and Patents Act 1988.

All rights reserved. No part of this publication may be reproduced, stored in a retrieval system, or transmitted in any form or by any means without prior permission in writing from the publisher.

First published in 2021 by Hunt Press.

First published in Great Britain.

All characters are fictitious and any resemblance to real persons, living or dead, is purely coincidental.

JOIN THE HUNTING PARTY

Get a FREE, Stirling Hunt Mission, top-secret psychological profile and short story.

Based on true events.

Just tell me where to send it: details in the back of the book.

For Ema

A scrimmage in a Border Station-
A canter down some dark defile
Two thousand pounds of education
Drops to a ten-rupee *jezail*.

- RUDYARD KIPLING, ARITHMETIC ON THE FRONTIER

AFGHANISTAN
MAP WITH KEY POINTS OF INTEREST

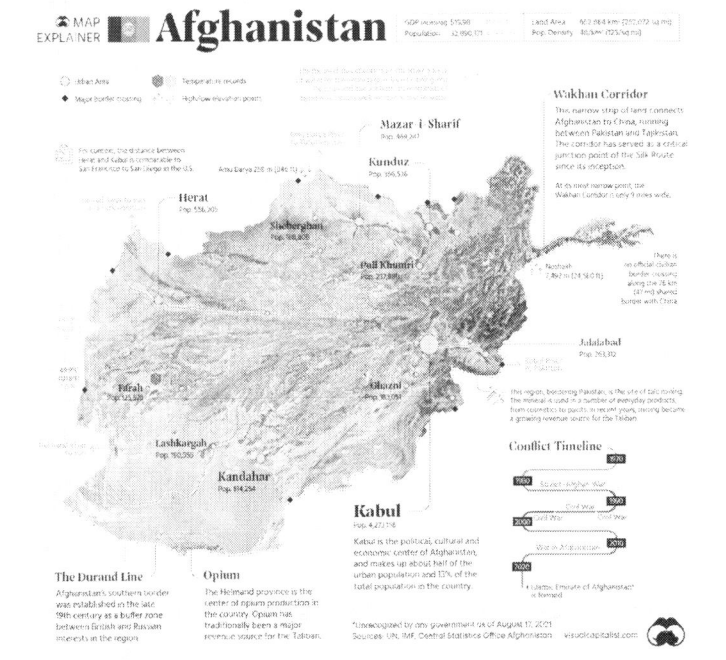

Afghanistan

GDP (nominal): $19.8B
Population: 32,890,171
Land Area: 652,864 km² (252,072 sq mi)
Pop. Density: 48.08/km² (125/sq mi)

- Urban Area
- Major border crossing
- Temperature records
- High/low elevation points

Wakhan Corridor
This narrow strip of land connects Afghanistan to China, running between Pakistan and Tajikistan. The corridor has served as a critical junction point of the Silk Route since its inception.

At its most narrow point, the Wakhan Corridor is only 9 miles wide.

Mazar-i-Sharif
Pop. 469,247

Kunduz
Pop. 356,536

For centuries, the distance between Herat and Kabul is comparable to San Francisco to San Diego in the U.S.

Amu Darya 258 m (846 ft)

Herat
Pop. 556,205

Sheberghan
Pop. 160,000

Pul-i-Khumri
Pop. 220,000

There is no official civilian border crossing along the 76 km (47 mi) shared border with China.

Noshakh 7,492 m (24,580 ft)

Jalalabad
Pop. 263,312

Farah
Pop. 125,500

Ghazni
Pop. 181,094

This region, bordering Pakistan, is the site of talc mining. The mineral is used in a number of everyday products, from cosmetics to paints. In recent years, mining became a growing revenue source for the Taliban.

Lashkargah
Pop. 160,250

Kandahar
Pop. 614,254

Conflict Timeline
- 1970
- 1980 Soviet-Afghan War
- 1990 Civil War
- 2000 Civil War
- 2010 War in Afghanistan
- 2020 "Islamic Emirate of Afghanistan" is formed

Kabul
Pop. 4,273,156

Kabul is the political, cultural and economic center of Afghanistan, and makes up about half of the urban population and 15% of the total population in the country.

The Durand Line
Afghanistan's southern border was established in the late 19th century as a buffer zone between British and Russian interests in the region.

Opium
The Helmand province is the center of opium production in the country. Opium has traditionally been a major revenue source for the Taliban.

*Unrecognized by any government as of August 17, 2021
Sources: UN, IMF, Central Statistics Office Afghanistan visualcapitalist.com

CHAPTER ONE

Cairo, Egypt

HUNT DECIDED a long time ago that he wouldn't make it to his thirtieth birthday. Now he thought he might not make it past this afternoon.

He sat on a springy single bed, he could feel the rough itchiness of the blankets under his *thobe*. He was dressed in the traditional white robe that Muslim men wore. He stared at himself in the stained mirror opposite his bed. It had a crack running across it that split his face in half. He didn't recognise himself. His eyes looked angry. He had a permanent scowl. And he'd put it to good effect.

His heart was beating like he'd just finished the hundred yard dash, but it wasn't nerves. He wasn't nervous about it. It was an intense feeling. Like standing on the edge of a bridge and preparing to jump. He was on the cusp of achieving a goal. Not just a goal, achieving an obsession.

He'd made up his mind that he had nothing left to live for, and that the love of his life deserved more than the violent death she'd gotten. Now he only had something to kill for.

He wasn't feeling nervous because he was resigned to his fate. His mind, body, and soul were aligned. He had only one, simple, central goal. Justice.

He had no ambitions to escape. He'd tracked down a link into a terror cell called the Egyptian Islamic Jihad, and the man the authorities wanted but couldn't get. And now he was going to do something that neither the United States government and its allies seemed willing to do, or incapable of doing. He was about to walk into a viper's nest of Islamic extremists and execute their leader.

He was dressed like they dressed. Looked like they looked. And spoke like they spoke. Thick elongated beard, dark hair, an olive tan. The only thing that gave him away as a westerner were his grey eyes that looked out from those two angry slits.

He'd replayed this moment over and over in his mind. He visualised it every day and every night. He was on the cusp of his objective. So why was he feeling so agitated? He wanted to succeed. More than anything, he wanted to kill this man. The man he was after had taken the only thing in the world he cared about, and the only thing he considered happiness, and light, and joy. Now it was all dark for him. Only this thing mattered.

He knew that if he was caught he would be severely beaten, tortured, and eventually killed. The thought of dying didn't scare him, the only thing that scared him was not being successful ... Failure. Failing her.

He didn't care what anyone else thought. He didn't care if they wondered *how* somebody could do such a thing? All he cared about was that they suffered, like he suffered. That they felt the loss like he felt it. That they saw first-hand the pain that they caused in the name of an evil, unholy war.

His target went by many aliases: Abu Muhammad, Abu Fatima, Muhammad Ibrahim, Abu Abdallah, Abu al-Mu'iz, The Doctor, The Teacher, Nur, Ustaz, Abu Mohammed Nur al-Deen, and Abdel Muaz.

His real name was Dr. Ayman al-Zawahiri. He masterminded the bloody, synchronised August bombings of the United States embassies in the East African cities of Dar es Salaam, Tanzania, and Nairobi, Kenya.

Hunt had been in the first year of his Doctorate, reading Economics at the University of Cape Town, South Africa. He stayed on for postgraduate studies, because he was trying to qualify for the Olympics as a rower, and this was his final shot before the real world kicked in and the obligations started.

In the first few weeks of that school year he met a tall, athletic and beautiful American girl called Kelly Armstrong, from Harvard. She was in her fourth year of a degree in Politics and had come on exchange to Cape Town, South Africa, to volunteer, play soccer, and study. She wanted more than anything to join the Peace Corps. She had full lips, a great laugh, beautiful round eyes, and long curly hair that couldn't be tamed. Her hair was just like her spirit.

Hunt was in love. The real, life changing, carefree love of youth. He'd never seen anything like her. They'd been introduced through a friend, met in the local student pub and he'd walked her home. He asked if he could kiss her. The moment he felt her soft, full lips, his life as he knew it was over.

They were happy. He was happier than he'd ever thought possible, because he never considered the possibility of being so happy. Later that year Hunt proposed. He didn't have money for a ring, so he sanded down and varnished a piece of driftwood. He'd collected it during one of their sunset strolls on Camps Bay beach. The thin, lightly varnished-yellow ring had made her happier than he'd seen anyone in his life. It was romantic and they were in love. He promised, one day, he'd get her a diamond.

Days after the engagement, Hunt was in her dorm room. He saw the letter she'd left open on her desk. First, he noticed the U.S. government insignia in the header. He picked it up and read it. It was an offer. A chance to work for the Peace Corps at the U.S. Embassy in Tanzania. She walked in on him and saw the single tear run down his cheek. They stood and looked at one another. She ran to him and they hugged. They knew. They both cried. Said they would stay together. He would visit her and join her as soon as he could. He drove her to the airport and she cried again. This time he just about held it together. He'd managed to hold it together until he was on the drive home, that's when it hit him and he had to pull over. He couldn't drive through the frustration and the tears.

She'd been in Tanzania for less than six weeks. Hunt was lecturing a group of first year students when his phone vibrated. He glanced at the screen. American number. He answered.

"She's dead," Bill Armstrong told him. Kelly's father didn't say anything else. The two men had never met, but Hunt could tell he was a strong man, who loved his family, worked hard for them every day. And now his beautiful daughter was gone. He'd said everything he could ever say about it.

Hunt went back to his apartment and watched it on the news. A white plume of smoke rose up from the destroyed frontage of the embassy. The terrorists had detonated a bomb inside a petrol tanker just after most people had arrived for work. Cars burned in the streets. Trees were toppled. The heat from the blast hit a packed commuter bus full of hard working, ordinary people. They were incinerated on their way to provide for their children. Americans died. Kelly, his fiancée, was one of them.

Hunt left the next night. He didn't take anything with him. The suspects were from Egypt. He bought a ticket to Cairo and disappeared. No one knew where he was. And no one in Cairo knew *who* he was.

He spent time in the markets. He practised Arabic. He bought Egyptian clothes. He sat at shisha bars and spoke to locals. He enrolled in Arabic classes. He asked for introductions. He made friends with dishwashers and chefs. They took him to their mosque. He spoke about converting to Islam with the *imam*. He became well known in the neighbourhood. People liked him.

One day, after proving himself, he recited a short declaration standing in front of the faithful in the mosque. He committed to follow Islam for life and submit to the will of *Allah*. He volunteered in the community. He taught lessons to boys in a shelter. Then, one of the dishwashers at the St. Regis introduced him to an angry looking young man. Hunt had made it widely known that he had money. He'd made it known that he was angry at the west. And he'd made it known that he supported the cause of Islamic Jihad. It had taken many months, first to learn, then to gain acceptance, and finally to understand the nuance. No one in the Arabic world says what they mean. The true meaning is in what they don't say, not in what they do.

He had an interview with a blind old man in a dingy office. He answered questions on the *Quran*. He spoke in Arabic. He told of his devotion to the cause. How *Allah* had chosen him in a dream. He told them he wanted more than anything to meet with the leader of the movement. To be a *martyr*. The old man took him on. Showed him how to make bombs in a way that, when they blew up, would kill people.

Almost a year after walking out on his life, he was within

minutes of a meeting with Doctor al-Zawahiri, and he planned to get close enough to use the sharpened spoke of a bicycle wheel to stab him in the heart. Failing that, he'd sewed a suicide vest, which he wore under his white robes. If the shank didn't work, or he couldn't get close enough to his target, he would detonate the two cut-down empty ice-cream containers he'd filled with Semtex. They were packed full of nails, ball bearings, and glass. Hunt wore homemade claymores on his chest and on his back.

The meeting was for a small cell of the faithful. They were gathering to hear from their leader. They were gathering to be recruited into the holy war against America. Hunt was ready to die if it meant that no-one else had to. If it meant he took as many terrorists with him as he could. If it meant he could give them some of their own bitter bile to swallow. See how confident they were in their faith.

Maybe his act would bring some peace to Kelly's parents. Knowing their daughter's murderer received a trial by fire. It was nearly time for the meeting. He was to walk to the market. There, the group would be taken from the blind man's basement to a secret location. They would be introduced to the Doctor. Hunt was ready. His grey eyes stared out from under his bushy eyebrows, thick beard, and white-knitted *kufi* cap. It was all for her. If heaven existed, he planned on being with her soon.

CHAPTER TWO

HUNT HEARD a knock on the door. He turned to look at it. It didn't open.

"Just one second," he said in Arabic.

There was no other sound. He stood and quickly went to his wardrobe. He pulled on a cloak over the top of his thobe. He checked himself in the mirror and made sure the bulge was not too big at the back. Hunt walked to the door. He pulled it open a crack. It was the mother of the family whose house he was staying in. They were close to the mosque and the community and Hunt paid them a small amount of money to rent a room in their home.

"Excuse me, Mister, your friend Fahim is at the front door," she said.

Hunt thanked her and she stepped back from the door. Hunt left the room and left the door open. He had nothing to hide. He felt her watching him as he descended the staircase. He glanced back at her and she gave him a thin, concerned smile. He waved his hand from his waist. A small gesture of thanks. He doubted he would ever see her again. He doubted she would ever outlive the controversy of having hosted a western assassin. After all, that was what he was, wasn't it? An executioner of justice. He'd taken it upon himself to find those responsible. And now he was taking it upon himself to put an end to it.

Hunt went to the front door. He saw the shape of a man standing behind the glass. The figure was distorted by the patterns in the panes of glass. Hunt pulled open the front door and saw Fahim. He was a thin, wiry chap with a wispy moustache and not much facial hair around his chin. The other boys at the centre teased him mercilessly and Fahim was very angry inside. Hunt knew that Fahim thought of him as a way to channel his anger and live vicariously through someone like him. Hunt had the physicality, and he imposed himself on situations. Fahim saw how the others reacted to him, like he was a leader, and he was so proud to be friends with a man who had left his home, thousands of miles away, and travelled to Cairo to join the cause.

Hunt greeted him in the customary manner. It was not unusual for Egyptian men to hold hands. And Fahim held onto Hunt's hand longer than he would've felt comfortable in any other setting.

"My brother," Fahim said.

"My brother," Hunt replied.

They walked down the street towards the market. Fahim was excited and spoke a lot about what they could expect and who they would meet. Hunt was wary. His eyes scanned. He was weighed down by the bomb in the vest and he was hot under the robe. Fahim couldn't understand why he was dressed like that, but Hunt made an excuse that the mother at the house thought that he would get sick and wanted him to wrap up warmly. She was worried about him, he said. Fahim laughed, but there was no arguing with an Egyptian mother.

Hunt and Fahim started moving through the crowds and

they tightened like a knot in a rope. They approached the market and there were more people. They bumped into him and to got in his way. Hunt protected his front and tried not to be paranoid about detonating the plastic explosive. The last thing he wanted was to blow himself up in a crowded market by accident.

Just then, two blacked out SUVs broke cover from the alleyways on either side of the road, the tyres locked and kicked up dust and skidded to a halt in front of each other. The doors opened and men in dark glasses and blue jeans jumped down from the vehicles. They lifted black 9mm pistols and pointed them at Hunt and Fahim. They turned to run. As they turned, two more black SUVs cut across their path of escape. The doors opened and more men climbed down and held weapons.

Fahim turned and looked at Hunt. He grabbed Hunt's arm and said quickly, "My brother, they have found us. The Americans! You must get away. You must save yourself! You are very important to the cause."

Fahim was scared. Hunt was annoyed. One of the agents lifted his wrist to his mouth and said into a mic, "We've got him. We've got the guy. It's him."

The same agent then dropped his hand from his mouth and yelled, "Get down! Get down on the ground now, hands behind your back! Do not move. Do not move! Get down."

Hunt and Fahim dropped slowly to their knees.

"Hands behind your head! Interlock your fingers. Lie face down in the sand. Face in the sand. Do it!"

Hunt was hesitant to put too much weight on the vest and on his chest. Fahim did what he was told. The same agent looked through the sight of his Glock and yelled instructions at Hunt. Hunt couldn't tell them that he was strapped with enough Semtex to destroy half the buildings on the street.

He couldn't let Fahim know that he was ready to destroy

the brotherhood. Fahim would know right away that Hunt was a liar. Someone who had infiltrated their circle. Fahim would be responsible. He'd been the one who'd vouched for Hunt.

One of the agents grabbed Fahim from behind by the wrists and pulled him up and away. They manhandled him into one of the other vehicles. Hunt glanced over his shoulder as they did. He saw them tie Fahim's hands with cable-ties and put an empty hessian sack over his head. There were muffled cries and then they slammed the back doors shut. Silence. The agent covering Hunt lifted his free hand and touched his ear. He listened for a moment, and then said loudly to his colleagues over his shoulder, "We've gotta get out of here! Bogeys closing in."

"Sir ..." Hunt said. He was calm. It was actually kind of funny to him. Now, of all the times, this was when they decided to do it.

"Not now, boy. Get on the ground!"

"Sir, there is something I have to tell you. I'm not sure you're going to be too pleased." Hunt could see by the agent's reaction that he was confused about something. Hunt had even picked up an Arabic-accented slant to his English. Just some of the changes Hunt had gone through, physically, to become a friend of Islamic terrorists.

"I'm wearing a suicide vest," Hunt said. "I have an improvised explosive device strapped to my chest. If I lie down, I am worried it's going to explode."

"Jesus Christ! Son, what the hell are you doing?" the agent said and holstered his pistol. The agent went over to Hunt and lifted him from under his armpit.

"What've you got, a pressure switch?" the agent asked.

"Yes, sir," Hunt said.

The agent got on the network and told the vehicle holding Fahim to leave the scene. He took Hunt to the back of the waiting SUV. Once Fahim's vehicle had driven off, the American turned to Hunt.

"That thing gonna detonate the moment you take it off?" he asked.

Hunt hoped not. "No, sir, I don't think so."

"You don't think?"

Hunt shook his head.

"No, you don't think so. Jesus. What a moron."

Hunt dropped his head. He felt like a moron, frustrated and pissed off.

"Right, clear the area! Create a cordon. And get me an EOD now!"

Hunt waited. The Egyptian military kept the cordon. The Explosive Ordnance Disposal technicians arrived and removed the device from Hunt's shoulders.

"He was really going to do it," the technician said to the American as he walked away.

They handcuffed Hunt and put a sack over his head.

"You better not move around too much in there then," the agent said and pushed his head down so he fit into the back seat. "We're liable to shoot you."

The air-conditioning was on full. Hunt could hear the muffled complaints about the heat from the front seat. They drove at high speed and Hunt flopped around in the back seat, unable to brace for the sharp turns and jolts because of the sack over his head. It was a standard operational speed. Hunt knew they were foreign intelligence, or military intelligence, possibly Central Intelligence Agency, maybe Defence Intelligence Agency. He wasn't a hundred percent sure which.

They slowed. Hunt heard a quick, official greeting and the

grating of a metal gate. They accelerated hard and Hunt was thrown back into the seat. Then he felt the accelerator lift and the vehicle slowed, before the driver pressed hard on the brake and Hunt shot forward. The seatbelt caught him before he smacked his face against the headrest. The SUV skidded to a halt.

There were shouts and the doors opened. Hunt was grabbed and handled roughly. There were at least three men around him. He could smell their musky *eau de toilette* intermingled with their body odour. One of them smoked cigars. One liked to eat pistachios. They bundled him into a chair.

Two men grabbed each of his wrists and slammed them into a cold metal table. Hunt felt the restraints bite into his wrists as the handcuffs locked. They pulled the sandbag roughly off his head. He blinked and his eyes adjusted to the white light. He tried to rub his eyes but the chains grated and pulled tight against the table. You're in it now.

The men left the room. The door slammed shut. He couldn't even scratch his head where the hessian sack had rubbed against him. Hunt sat and waited. He heard some banging and some shouts echoing from far away. He had the distinct sensation that someone was watching him, but he didn't want to give them the satisfaction of looking at the one way glass to his left. After Hunt had sat in silence for what felt like an hour, and once he began to shiver from the cold, the heavy metal door clanked open again. Hunt looked up from the table.

The same agent as before walked in. He stood between the interview table and the door and took a sip of what smelled like weak coffee from a white plastic cup. He had sweat stains under his armpits and his brown hair stuck to his forehead. The heavy metal door slammed behind him and the agent jumped.

"It's enough to give you post-traumatic stress..." the agent said. Hunt was impassive.

The agent put the coffee down on the metal table, just out of reach, and stayed standing. Hunt wouldn't snatch at it anyway. He wasn't starving yet. The man reached into the back pocket of his jeans and pulled something out. It was a maroon, tatty passport. Hunt knew from the look if it that it was his. They'd been to the house. The agent tapped it on the palm of his hand like he was slapping a deck of cards.

He held it up and opened it and compared the picture to Hunt's face. He glanced between the picture and the bearded, tanned, angry looking face in front of him. Hunt realised his eyebrows were pressed together in a scowl and he looked away and relaxed his face. The passport picture of him showed a light-haired, fair-skinned, sixteen-year-old boy. The glint in his eyes gave the impression that he was full of the possibilities of life. Now, he felt tired, like he'd lived too many lives already.

"Hunt, Stirling James," the man said. Hunt looked at him. The man took a few steps forward and sat down in a chair, opposite Hunt, at the metal table. He sighed heavily as he sat. Hunt looked at the table. The seconds passed. The man leaned forward and said, "Hello?" and snapped his fingers a couple of times under Hunt's eyes.

Hunt looked up.

"Wakey-wakey, eggs and bakey," the man said. "Rise and shine, sunshine. I want to talk to you."

Hunt looked at him silently. Passive. He was in control of himself and his thoughts.

"Pretty darn catastrophic what's happened to you this morning, son. Don't ya think?"

Yes, it was, sort of. Could have been worse, could have been better. At least he wasn't dead. In relative terms, things were going pretty well, actually.

"It's all about context, I suppose," Hunt said.

"The hell does that mean?"

Hunt's voice had caught his interrogator off guard and he sat back and assessed his suspect for a few moments. Hunt reckoned that this guy must not have been expecting a collaborative suicide bomber. Do you know why we picked you up? Do you know who we are? Do you know what you're doing here? Hunt couldn't wait for the usual, long-winded interrogation to be over. He had things to do.

"Listen," Hunt said. "I don't know about you, but I've got many men to see about many different dogs ... So if we could move this along, I'd appreciate it."

"Somewhere else you'd rather be?" the agent said.

Hunt squinted at him. Curious thing to say. Yes, just a few. It was uninspired and Hunt just sighed loudly.

"I'm sorry, am I wasting your goddamn time?" the interrogator was frustrated.

Yes, yes you are, Hunt wanted to say. But, instead, he said nothing. He just smiled to himself. The agent was flustered.

"Listen, son, I don't know if you realise it or not but you're going to be in a world of pain. A world of pain. Unless, you cooperate ..."

Hunt wanted to laugh.

"Does this look like I'm not cooperating with you?" Hunt asked. "You haven't even asked me a question yet ... so, if we could skip ahead to that part, and get over whatever this is right now, that would be great."

"I know guys like you," the spook said, "I've *known* guys like you. It's you against the world, isn't it? Yeah, well, those guys don't last. Doesn't matter at what, they just don't. All that anger. All that, that, righteous indignation," he squinted as he said the word, "Pride is a very common vice, I believe. Those guys don't realise they need people. They don't realise they can't do it alone, until it's too late. And, what happens?

They can't see the thing that's right in front of their face, because they're too *goddamn* pissed off and too *goddamn* emotional to realise what's really going on. That they're really just hurting themselves more, and bringing the people around them down with them ... like the *friggin'* Titanic."

He was one of those Americans who didn't cuss too much. The agent glanced to his right into the one way mirror. They sat in silence. Hunt wasn't sure what to make of it. He didn't reply. He didn't say anything. The interrogator sighed like he was fighting a losing battle. The seconds passed and the large metal door opened again. Hunt heard men's shouts in Arabic echo down the corridor.

A tall, dark-skinned man in a grey suit strolled in. He held a manilla file in one hand. He was wiry-thin. He reminded Hunt of a Masai warrior without the face paint and giant earlobes. He walked forward. His high-shine black shoes reflected the fluorescent lighting and *clip-clopped* and scraped as the strode forward and then stopped. He dropped the file on the table and pushed it forward a few inches with his index finger.

The other agent slid his chair back and it grated on the tiled floor and he stood up. The black man sat. He interlocked his fingers and rested them on his lap. Here we go, Hunt thought.

CHAPTER THREE

The African-American interrogator lifted his index finger and waved it to and fro in Hunt's face. "Tell me, aaah," he said. "What kinda accent you got there?"

Hunt said nothing. There was a quiet moment.

"What do you got, huh? You see, me ..." the Maasai-looking man said. "I've got a bit of the southern drawl. You know? A bit of Tennessee mixed in there with my California-Stanford vibe, and then, you know, the Langley, Virginia ..."

He studied Hunt's eyes for reaction and then held them. He was relaxed. Like he and Hunt were new work colleagues having a chat. Shooting the breeze.

"Turns out you can tell a lot about a man from the way he speaks. So, what you got, huh? You see, I'm struggling to place it. You been in Egypt too long, that's for sure, 'cos you got the," he sideways glanced at his partner and then back at Hunt. Hunt felt the partner's eyes on him. In his peripheral vision he could see him as he leaned against the wall. The black man continued, "The, kind of, clipped and guttural gullet sounds they make when they say words like 'ghetto'. But, then, you've got what? The white-South African undertones. But, also it sounds a bit British, you know, not the east London *cockney-geezer* ... I'm talking about the Home Counties part of it."

He tapped his wide fingernail on the manilla file and said really slowly, drawing out every word, "Tell me, Mister whatever-your-real-name-is Hunt, what makes a university educated, olympic-level rower athlete, from South *Africa*, come over and sign up for a militant-fundamentalist-Islamic brotherhood of *jihad*, huh?"

The sentence clanged like a church bell and it echoed around in the silence that followed. Good question. Better question than he was expecting. Not bad for the first question of an interview. Not an easy one to answer either. Not an easy one to explain. Not one Hunt felt he should need to explain. Not one that was any of these people's business. He was doing what needed to be done.

"Gross incompetence on the part of the Central Intelligence Agency," Hunt said. "But, I'm just speculating, just based on those present you understand. I could be wrong, but you guys are really going to have to step your game up if you want to change my mind."

"Hot damn! The boy has a tongue on him," the grey-suited spook said and slapped his knee to emphasise the point. He looked at his colleague as he leaned against the wall and grinned. The colleague didn't look impressed. "Damn, son. You just tell it like it is, huh?"

Hunt sat still. Looked at his hands, they were turning purple in the restraints. He felt the metal biting into his skin. He knew this was patter.

"Uncomfortable here, isn't it?" the one against the wall said.

"Well, why don't you drop some more truth bombs on us?" the black guy followed up. "Tell us what you were doing here strapped with enough C-4 to bring down a city block ..."

"Semtex," Hunt said.

"Huh? I didn't catch that," the black guy leaned forward and cupped his hand behind his ear.

"You said C-4. It wasn't. It was Semtex."

"Oh!" he said and leaned back in his grey suit. "A chemist. Tell me more ..."

"And it's Rhodesia."

"Come again."

"Earlier. You said *South African*. I'm not. I'm Rhodesian."

"Uh-huh." the black guy said and looked at his colleague again. "And, that's in Africa, right?"

Hunt said nothing.

"Southern. Africa. Right?"

"Stop jerking us around," the standing guy said.

"Now that we know each other, at least, a little better ... why don't you tell us your story?"

"We don't know each other. You've identified me. You have a file on me and my passport. But you haven't identified yourselves. Or what jurisdiction you're holding me under."

They glanced at one another again and seemed like they were trying not to laugh. The black guy shook his head slowly and then reached inside his jacket pocket. He pulled out a thick, black-leather wallet. He tossed it towards Hunt's hands and it landed on the metal table with a thud.

"I'm Neills, this is Perkins," he said and lifted his chin to indicate his colleague up against the wall. The identification said they were from the Central Intelligence Agency. Hunt was in the deep end and sinking fast.

"Can I have my identification back?"

Hunt looked up and closed the wallet and tried to toss it to him. The chain clanked and the wallet wobbled and landed on the desk. Neills reached out and put it back in his jacket.

"So," Neills said and spread his hands, "Regale us."

Hunt thought about it for a moment. He looked directly into Neills' black pupils.

"You know what Islam means?" Hunt asked.

Neills shook his head.

"It literally translates as 'surrender to the will of God'."

"Yeah? What do I care, smart ass," Perkins said and shifted his butt from the wall and blew a raspberry at Hunt. "What does that translate directly as, huh? Smell my ass. That's what."

"As you can see, Mister Hunt, Perkins doesn't think much of your bullshit answer," Neills said with mock empathy.

"Yeah, well, that's the problem with you guys, isn't it? False confidence," Hunt said. Then he looked up and said loudly, "You've got a bunch of Islamist fanatics out that door who openly declared war against America. Six months later. *Six months*," Hunt pressed his finger into the metal table, "They killed *two hundred* people in coordinated strikes against American embassies abroad. And what have you done about it?" Hunt looked from one man to the other. He was genuinely asking. There was venom behind his eyes. The agents didn't answer. Neills waved a hand which told Hunt to go on.

"Yeah, I was a student. Yes, I was an athlete. Yes, I have a British passport ... so what?"

"Yes, you had a bomb strapped to your chest ..." Neills said.

Hunt looked at his purple hands again.

Neills turned and spoke to Perkins. "This is what I don't get," he indicated Hunt, "Here's a guy, smart guy." He reached forward and opened the file and read. "Post-graduate studies in Economics. Rower. World class. Look at this picture here," he held it up for Perkins to see. "Good looking young man. Young man who couldn't even buy a beer on United States soil. And yet, here he is, dressed like an *imam*, preaching about Islam and ready to commit suicide."

"Yup," Perkins said looking at Hunt, "It's a real head scratcher. I can't get my head around it either, boss."

"It's not that hard guys," Hunt said. "I just don't care if I die or not. You should try it. It's quite liberating. Yeah, I wanted the wife, car, white picket fence. Two point three kids. But, I don't *anymore*. I only want to live long enough to see al-Zawahiri dead."

Hunt looked at the agents one at a time. "He's here. In Cairo. Right now. al-Zawahiri is *here*. And *yet* you do nothing about it. Explain that to me ..."

"Bigger things to worry about," Neills said under his breath.

"Bigger things?" Hunt asked. He was dumbfounded. "Like what, the Y2K bug?"

"For one thing," Neills countered, "The year two-thousand bug is more important than some camel-screwing loudmouth -"

Hunt looked like he was about to tear the handcuffs from the desk and wrap them around Neills' face.

"We know he's here," Perkins said. "And, we heard on the grapevine that he was looking forward to capturing an infidel from Britain and strapping electrodes to your nuts until you squealed like the little piggy going all the way home."

Perkins pushed himself off the wall and sat down on the edge of the table. He was close to Hunt. Neills scooched the chair over and it grated on the floor once again.

"We need the Doctor *alive*," Perkins said. "End of story. There is more at play here than you could possibly fathom."

"Oh, yeah?" Hunt said and laughed. It was bitter. Laughing felt unnatural. "Sure, I'm sure it isn't just that you've totally underestimated the drive and divine purpose these people have. I'm sure it isn't just that, so far, these attacks have only happened in poor third-world places that the general American public couldn't give a single damn about."

Perkins looked at Hunt. Neills cleared his throat.

"What were you hoping to get out of it anyway?" Perkins asked. His tone was softer. "What were you thinking? You're just going to stroll in there and get your vengeance?"

Hunt took a deep breath. What else was there. What else did he have?

"You don't get it, man. I've got nothing else. I used to be a student, and I liked rowing, and reading, and going to the movies, and hanging out with girls. I had a fiancée, you know? I was pretty happy for somebody with the kind of loss that I've had in my life. But, I was *really* happy ..."

"Parents killed when you were little," Neills said, more for Perkins' benefit than to confirm that was what Hunt was referring to.

"But, that's all changed now," Hunt said.

Perkins glanced down at Neills. Hunt looked Perkins directly in the eye.

"Now," Hunt said. "I only care about one thing. Now, I only care about killing the man who took her from me. Who took her from her parents. That's it. That's all my life is now ... Okay? And you can't do anything about it. Besides kill me. You can kill me, or lock me up. But, the CIA, you guys," he pointed at them, "Don't kill people like me."

"Oh, no?" Perkins said with real surprise.

"No. You put me in play and you try and see how you can use me to affect the world in the way that you *want* it to be. I'm an instrument to you. But I'm not one that you can own. I only have one thing on my mind."

Neills stood and walked over to the one way glass. He had his hand on his hip and he wiped his mouth with the other. He watched Hunt in the reflection. Hunt glanced at him.

"So, what's it going to be? Firing squad, or, let me get this one terrorist for you, before he gets me?"

Neills turned from the mirror.

"That's never gonna happen, kid. Take some free advice. Give this whole charade up. It's not going to get you anywhere, 'cept maybe a prison cell or a body bag."

"Body bag, that's my guess," Perkins said and nodded in agreement and looked at Hunt. They had the routine down pat.

"If you really want to make a difference, or get this crap out of your system, you go to England on your British passport and you sign up to whichever unit you think is going to deploy first when the next war kicks off."

Neills walked to the door and banged on it. It opened and he walked out of the room. Perkins glanced quickly to see if he'd gone and went back to the table. He put both hands on the steel and leaned in close to Hunt's face and no more than whispered, "Listen to me son, this thing out there, it's a battle against an ideology that's bigger than us. It's bigger than the United States government. Any government. How do you defeat an idea. We *have* to do it together. If you really want to do this thing you think you want to do, you join the military and you do it together, with us. As a team. Your thing ... it's just one thing among thousands of other things. But, with your head on your shoulders, instead of your heart, you and *your* mind, you can help bring all of those thousands of things that affected so many thousands of people to a close. You can kill *all* the bastards ... but, you can't do it alone."

He stood up straight and stared at Hunt and then turned and walked out of the room.

CHAPTER FOUR

Late that night Neills sat alone in a dark office. He was still in his grey suit. He'd opened the collar and taken off his tie. He wasn't one to go in for local custom, but in his time in the Middle East he'd gotten into the habit of drinking tea. The Koshary tea was brewed black, with cane sugar and mint leaves. He found it light and refreshing. And the time it took to brew and the ceremony-like pour, from a tall pewter teapot, gave him pause.

He lifted the thimble-looking glass cup and sniffed the aromas and had a sip. He let the liquid linger and dilute. He set it down and picked up the telephone and pressed the numbers. He checked his watch as it rang. Knowing Soames he would still be in the office. It connected.

"A little fish swam straight into our net," Neills said. "And I immediately thought of you."

"How kind of you ..."

"We picked this kid up in the *bazaar*. One of yours. Idealistic as they come."

"Never mind," Soames said. "We'll soon turn him into a cynic. We always do. Why should he be of interest ... to us?"

His tongue-in-cheek humour sounded far away, but London was on their doorstep. The British Monarch used to own the Egyptian state. She became a new kind of Pharaoh. He probably thinks I don't understand the joke, Neills thought.

"Yeah," Neills said, acknowledging the question, and reached for his steaming cup of tea. The Brits had it right he thought as he took a sip. Something the Americans can't understand.

"We found something on his laptop."

Soames waited in silence. Neills set his tea down.

"Christ, what are you, keeping me in suspense ... What was it?" Soames asked.

After tea, Neills liked a smoke, he pulled out a crumpled soft pack of Queen Cleopatra cigarettes from his breast pocket. He lit one and took a deep inhale and leaned back in the chair as he exhaled. He heard Soames sigh and drum his fingers.

"Just don't forget who gave this to you, when the time comes," Neills said. These days it was the United States who really ran Egypt. He knew Soames knew it too.

"I won't forget who kept me hanging on, when the time comes ..." Soames replied.

Good one.

"This kid, he's green, but we found his records. Lots of meticulous records. Lists of names. Key players. Their profiles. Images. Everything. It was like God blessed us with a full intelligence set sent down to earth. Like he was writing a postdoctoral research paper and painting a picture of the entire underground network of players in Cairo."

"He sounds like a regular Picasso," Soames said.

"Van Gogh," Neills corrected him and took a drag. "Oil on canvas. It's a masterpiece."

"Well, whoever," Soames said willing to agree to disagree. "Share it with us and I will tell you how good it really is ..."

"No," Neills said and tapped the ash. "Maybe I can when the time comes. But we caught him, we get to hang the picture on the wall. I'll give you the next best thing, though."

"Oh, yes? You're a regular Santa Claus."

"The artist. We're releasing him back into the pond. So you can catch him, if you like. If you *can*. Now, I'm not saying whether you should or not, but I am giving you this courtesy call, because I think he'll be of interest to you."

"All right," Soames said.

How about a thank you, you limey prick? Neills tapped the ash again.

"That it?" Neills asked.

"What do you want, a written bloody note?"

Neills shook his head and exhaled out the side of his mouth and mashed the end of the cigarette into his ashtray. He ran his palm over the top of the desk to wipe away sprinkles of ash.

"Send the file and one of my guys will take a look," Soames said.

"You'd better be fast. He's on his way back to you now. Bought and paid for by the United States of America's taxpayer, so be grateful."

"So you're sending us your garbage again? And I suppose you're going to want me to feel grateful. We send our dirty nappies and rotting vegetables to the Philippines to deal with, but I don't think they feel lucky about it. Grow up. Bloody yank."

"Posh twot," Neills said and slammed down the phone.

He leaned back in his chair and chuckled. The chuckle turned into a laugh. And then he was shaking as the laugh ran through his whole body. What an English prat. Neills had played his hand. Hunt's future now lay with the Secret Intelligence Service of the United Kingdom. No doubt he would be pinged and picked up the moment he passed through the border at Heathrow.

CHAPTER FIVE

London, England

Colour Sergeant Edwin E. Ewing of the Staffordshire Regiment sat behind a light-coloured, prefabricated wooden desk. It had sharp corners and bits of the chipboard were exposed and flaked onto the industrial carpet. His navy blue beret was rolled up and sat on the top corner of his desk. He wore working dress. British Army issue camouflage pattern uniform otherwise known as DPM.

Disruptive Pattern Material. It was dark browns and blacks and greens. Selected in advance of the expected Russian land invasion of Western Europe. If he sat still enough in the dim recruiting office people just walked by him without noticing the twenty-year infantry veteran with tours of Bosnia, Northern Ireland, and the Gulf. As he sat there, flicking through a tabloid newspaper, which he read by moving his mouth, and trying hard not to keep looking at page three, he felt an onrush of panicked anxiety.

He was getting out of the army in exactly twenty-seven days, eleven hours, fifty-nine minutes and fifty-nine seconds. He couldn't sleep from the thought of it. He was closer to forty than thirty and had spent the whole of his adult life, and some of his childhood, in the armed forces. He didn't know anything besides and it made him more afraid than he'd ever been about the prospect of deploying to dilapidated hot spots around the world.

Colour Ewing looked up from his paper as the automatic door clunked and folded open on itself. The little light that managed to enter the basement-like recruiting office was blocked like an eclipse of the sun. Ewing squinted and saw the silhouette of a man's body framed by the rectangular doorway. The guy hadn't seen Colour Ewing sitting there, because he seemed to be having a conversation with himself. He half-turned to leave and then stopped. Then he turned back and looked into the office again. He must have seen the Colour Sergeant this time. And Ewing called out, "Help you?"

The guy dropped his head for a second, then lifted it, then entered the office. Ewing was impressed. The size of him. He looked lean, but with power. He wandered in and looked at all the recruiting posters of university aged kids having a great time on the walls. All sun, sea, and snow. A few with cadets and officers looking proud while standing on parade. One poster had a guy charging with bayonet fixed.

"Hi there son, can I help you?"

The lad looked tired. Eyes were bloodshot. Short-cropped birch-coloured hair in need of a wash. Clean shaven. Square jaw and jaw muscles that pulsed metronomically. His face looked like it was chiselled out of granite by a sculptor who had skill but no time. He held a single nylon duffel bag in his left hand and looked down at Ewing.

"Ah, yes please. I think I'd like to join the forces. Sign up for the forces ..."

"You think?"

The lad looked back at Ewing. Impassive. A look that told him he wasn't going to put up with a hard time.

"Take a seat," the Colour said and pointed to the maroon chair in front of his desk. The guy sat down, sat still, and looked at the posters on the wall behind Ewing's desk again. Then he stood and chose an information booklet from the flyer stand and sat down again.

"Which of the services are you interested in joining?"

"I'm not sure."

"All right. Well, maybe I can help with that. First, I am going to need some details from you."

Colour Ewing pulled a clipboard from his desk drawer.

"Name?"

"Hunt, Stirling James."

"First name, Stirling. Last name, Hunt," Ewing said out loud as he scribbled the name down.

"Address, contact information?"

Hunt shook his head.

"Are you staying somewhere?"

"No."

Ewing looked up at him for a second and then put the pen and clipboard down.

"Listen," he said and checked the form, "Stirling, I am going to need a little more. You know? This is a professional armed forces. People who want to be there."

"I know."

"Where are you from?"

The guy raised his eyebrows, "Not from around here ..." he said and sighed.

"No, that's for sure. You look a little tired, son. Do you just need a place to sleep for a few hours?"

"No, I, ah, just got off a long flight. Overnight. Wasn't very comfortable; I didn't sleep."

"Yeah, I haven't been sleeping too well myself. I know how that feels ... What was it, guy in front's chair squishing your legs?"

"Something like that," Hunt said and forced a grin. He sat forward and rested his elbows on his knees and rubbed his eyes with the base of his palm.

"Why'd you want to sign up then?"

"To kill bad guys ..."

Colour Ewing sat silent. Hunt stopped rubbing his eyes and looked up at him. Ewing had never heard someone say it out loud like that before. Just like that. Straight shot, out in the open. Never heard it. Even if they were thinking it, most people were young kids, came in all nervous and thinking they had to behave like they were in the army already. All, yes-sir, no-sir, from the get go. Not this guy. He seemed uncompromisingly honest.

"Which will be the next regiment or unit, or whatever, to be going on operations, to deploy?" Hunt asked.

Ewing thought for a second, "I'm not sure, son. It doesn't really work like that."

"Okay, well who would you put your money on deploying first, when the proverbial hits the fan?"

"Paras and Marines are always a good shout for that. You could always join the Special Air Service, or Special Boat Service, from either of those two. Those lads are always deploying all over the world. But, it's tough. You have to want it."

Hunt said nothing.

"Well, who's the best out of those?"

"I mean, I'm going to be biased, aren't I? But, if I was

being honest, I'd say the navy lads probably have the edge. I always preferred the water me; anyways. Not sure why I joined the Staffords," Ewing said and smiled a bit wryly and forlornly.

"Why's that?"

"Oh, I don't know, 'spose I like sailing. Not that I've ever been mind -"

"Sorry, I mean, why is the Special Boat Service better than the SAS?"

"Well, for one thing, you never hear anything about them. Not a peep. Makes me think there is something more to it, you know? Everyone knows the SAS lads in their black gear fast-roping into embassies. How 'secret' and 'special' is that?"

Hunt shrugged.

"Whereas you'd never even heard of the SBS before, am I right? And they're never in the papers, like the SAS are. They're the real deal ..."

"Yeah, but the whole world is afraid of the SAS ..." Hunt said.

"Are they? Yeah, well, but who are they SAS afraid of then ...?"

"The Special Boat Service," Hunt said. He smiled for the first time.

"Okay. I'll tell you what," Colour Sergeant Ewing said. "You give me your passport. You go away and fill in this form," he handed Hunt a thick cream-coloured booklet.

Hunt reached out and took it reluctantly.

"Don't look so pleased," Ewing said. "I've got to do it too. Get you loaded onto the system. No mean feat when you've got all the IT skills of a circus trained macaque, like me."

Hunt looked at the lines and lines of tiny boxes and dashed lines in which to write.

"Once you finish that," Ewing continued, "Go through to the computer room, over there," he pointed behind the desk, "You're going to need to do a few aptitude tests, to see if you meet the base criteria, psychologically, emotionally, and numerically."

Hunt said nothing.

"And believe me if I can do it, then you, sure as a bull has massive balls can too."

While Hunt went off to fill in the paperwork and click through the tasks on the computer, and write an essay, Ewing fired up his desktop computer and got comfortable. He scanned the keyboard with his index finger looking for the letters and pressed them one at a time as he came across them. As he sat there working his way through the alphabet each time, he muttered to himself, "Wasn't bloody trained for this ... fire a mortar, no problem ... emergency casevac, bring it on ... bloody hell," he would sigh and look at the ceiling.

"Form filling nonse -" Colour Sergeant Ewing jumped when a sudden red box flashed on his screen. He'd just inputted Hunt's passport information. He was terrified he'd done something wrong. The monitor was frozen and it wouldn't let him do anything. He pressed the mouse several times randomly clicking it on the screen and bashed the keyboard against the table, but nothing worked. He read the box as it flashed on the screen. It was in black writing against a red background which made it difficult for him to read through his dyslexia. It told him to call a number. The person identified by the system was a person of interest.

"The bloody hell does that mean?" Ewing said. He scribbled down the number and left his station to go and make the call in a private room.

"Hi, I'm calling because of an alert on my screen ..."

"What was the reference to the dialogue?"

Ewing read it out to them.

"Who is calling, and in what context has the alert been recorded?"

Ewing told them who he was and what he was doing with Stirling Hunt.

"Okay. All noted. I will cancel the alert now and you can proceed with your business. Stay near the phone in-case we need to contact you."

"All right, but who the hell are you and what is this about?" Ewing asked. The line went dead and he stared at the receiver.

Hunt came out of the computer room looking at the beige booklet of forms in his hand. Ewing was still feeling a bit confused and a bit lost. He scratched his head and wondered whether he should mention it. Probably better not to.

"All done?" he called out cheerfully.

"I think so," Hunt said, equally falsely-cheerful. "What's wrong?" Hunt asked.

Ewing realised he must have been able to read it on his face. He quickly moved some papers around and got busy with something to look more energetic and upbeat.

"Right well, let me pull your scores up here. See if you're a fit ..."

Ewing punched the keys and then sat and stared at the screen.

"What is it?" Hunt asked.

Ewing mouthed the numbers and then checked them again.

"I've never seen anything like it," he said quietly. "What did you say you did again?"

Hunt pursed his lips and just shook his head.

"You've passed with flying colours. *More* than flying colours. The system is recommending I talk to you about becoming a helicopter pilot. It's a really exciting time right now to be an Apache pilot."

Hunt shook his head again. "No thanks. I want to be a Royal Marine. Regular grunt."

"But, you aren't ... *aaah*," Colour Ewing dropped his thought while double-checking the numbers on his monitor. "You certainly should apply to go in as an officer, either army or navy."

"No thanks," Hunt said. "I just want to be a grunt. The basic training is shorter, right?"

Ewing nodded. Hunt was right.

"Well then I want to apply for selection as soon as possible."

"Selection? So the man who knew nothing two hours ago is now an expert?"

Hunt shrugged.

"Listen," Ewing said and gave Hunt a look. Like he was serious. Like Hunt was seeing the real Ewing, the boy who'd signed up all enthusiastic and naive as a sixteen-year old, without better prospects of putting food in his mouth.

Hunt wasn't seeing the professional Colour Sergeant persona anymore. His face relaxed and he looked at Hunt like he was the boy who didn't know anything. "You might be smart," Ewing said, "but you might also be *too* smart. Smart guys like you can see all the details in the world. All the pieces of the spider web. Like how you can see it when the sun shines through a web in the morning, where it connects, how intricate it is. Guys like you can recognise the pattern, but sometimes you miss the basic stuff. You miss the bigger picture. You miss the *sun* shining down, while you're looking at it glinting off the web."

Hunt's face screwed up trying to decipher what the soon-to-be-retired non-commissioned recruitment officer was trying to say. It riled Colour Sergeant Ewing up, but he stayed in the mode of the boy soldier and looked back at Hunt. He was just trying to impart his one fundamental base principle, or life lesson, that he'd learned after his nearly-forty years.

"I did some reading," Hunt said. "So, when can I get started ...?"

"Oh, you did some *reading* ..." Ewing said. He said it in high note and filled it to the brim with contempt. "I'm trying to tell you there is no going back. Right now, you have a choice. I don't know what you are into. In *for*. But, - and no matter what it is - you can choose different. Once you sign on that dotted line and commit, for someone like you, it's over. They've got you forever."

"I could still choose to get out, down the line ..." Hunt said.

"Because 'you read it'?" Ewing said and shook his head. "You might have read it, but you don't get it though. Do you really think after all that they invest in you, you're just going to get to retire someplace warm? Right now, son, you are looking into the abyss and it's drawing you in. You want to go in there ... because it *wants* you in there. You are falling head first into the war machine ... the abyss of the *state-run* war machine. There's no gettin' out. Believe me. They lock your mind in." He tapped the side of his head. Ewing was quiet for a minute as he saw Hunt realise there was one way out.

"Except for dying ..." Hunt said.

"Except for dying, then you get out? Nah," Ewing said. "You'll be buried - *if* you're buried - you'll still be in their boneyard. A nice military one where young recruits go to visit you once a year to see first hand their retirement plots. A place where the bones are kept. A brotherhood of the willing, even in death. Is that what you want? To be part of a brotherhood? One you need to make sacrifices for. Sacrifices like your life ..."

"I appreciate the sentiment, Colour Sergeant, I really do. Believe me ..." Hunt said.

"But ..." Ewing cocked his head and looked at Hunt with a blank stare.

"... If you knew anything about me, you'd know that I am ready to make that sacrifice."

"Fine. But, do you want to? And, would you be making that sacrifice for your mates, the blokes who are in the shit with you, to give your life that they may have theirs? Or, is it for yourself? That you would sacrifice your own life, for *you*," he jabbed his index finger out as he made the point, "And *not* for *them*?"

Silence.

"Because, you are right. I might not know you. The *real* you. Whatever the bleedin' hell that means ... I see a guy doing this for himself. Not for others. That isn't duty and sacrifice. It's selfishness and carelessness."

Hunt poked his tongue into his cheek and gave Ewing the same blank stare.

"How about tomorrow?" Hunt asked.

"Tomorrow? What, to join the Royal Navy? No, son."

"When then?"

"This is going to take at least a few months. Six minimum. Long process -"

"Christ," Hunt said as he leaned back in the maroon desk chair and covered his face with his hands. "Six months! You can't be serious. I could invent a training course for myself in less time than it takes to apply."

"That's the way the system is ..." Ewing said. "But, maybe it's good to have a break, think it over, be sure you don't want to do something more individualistic, like be a helicopter pilot. Believe me, I was a grunt for a long time, and those flyboys live the high life. No pun intended."

"No," Hunt said and stood and grabbed his application form from the desk. "Sorry for wasting your time. This isn't something that can wait." He picked up his half-full duffel bag.

"Probably for the best. Where will you go?"

"I'm not sure. To invent a training course. Thailand, probably. Those guys have a brutal fighting system and I want to learn. Then, maybe the eastern bloc. Sure I can find some ex-KGB *Spetsnaz* guys to teach me weapons."

Ewing wasn't impressed, but he remembered the strange phone call and thought he'd better at least keep the intelligence.

"At least leave your application forms with me, in case you change your mind? I can submit them for you remotely, if you do."

"I won't."

"Well, you never know. Leave them ..." Ewing tapped the desk and then held out his hand. Hunt glanced at them and relented and pushed them into Ewing's outstretched hand. "How do I contact you?" Ewing asked.

Hunt pulled out a small mobile phone. A burner he'd bought in an underground station kiosk. Hunt slid the phone across the desk and Ewing read the number on the screen and scribbled it down.

"And here, take mine," the Colour Sergeant held out his card for Hunt to take. "I'm only here a few more weeks, but call me if you have a change of heart. I'll submit the paperwork ..."

Hunt stood there for a long time, just looking at Ewing holding out his business card. Ewing's shoulder got sore and started to tire and he shifted in his seat. Then, swiftly, Hunt snatched the card. He looked down at it and said, "You know what, screw it, submit the paperwork. If they want me, they know how to get in touch. I'm going to Thailand for six months, so check the time difference before you call. I don't want to be woken in the middle of the night ... I might be busy," Hunt winked.

He turned and walked out in just the same manner as he'd come in, like a gunslinger pushing through the swinging saloon doors, his frame blocking out all the light coming into the building as he passed.

He turned in the doorway and said, "Don't worry Colour Sergeant, I won't let any of the blokes down, you know? I am doing this for selfish reasons. But, I want to be the best at whatever I can do to keep people safe. That includes the people I will be working with. Okay? You won't regret it."

Hunt walked out into the sunshine. Ewing checked his watch and wondered whether he should call the number again.

CHAPTER SIX

Phuket, Thailand

A few months later

Hunt twisted his torso and spun his right leg in a wide-arching side kick. The Muay Thai trainer braced himself by squishing up his face and half-ducked out of the way. Hunt's shin, ankle and foot slammed into the pad and it whip-cracked on impact.

There was an echoey slap and grunt all around him in the fight gym. Hunt'd been there nearly three months and always drew a crowd to his ring when he sparred or hit the pads. He was lean, his stomach muscles tight, and sweat dripped off him. The gym was an open sided metal barn. Under the persistent Phuket sun it was like training in a hotbox. Hunt went through two gallons of water every training session. A whistle blew.

"Thirty pushups, thirty sit ups, ten seconds rest!" the lead trainer yelled. Hunt got down and on his fists and started doing push-ups with his hands inside the boxing gloves. He counted out the repetitions.

"One, two, three ..."

"Stir-leen!" the instructor called out, still holding his whistle near his mouth.

"Yeah?" Hunt said in-between push-ups. "Four, five, six, seven ..."

"Phone call! You come now."

Hunt got up and ducked out of the ring. Sweat dripped onto the canvas floor. He'd had months of early morning starts and had done three training sessions a day, six days a week. He'd run from his flat to the gym, do the regulation push-ups and sit-ups for the Marines - a hundred sit-ups and a hundred pushups - with two minutes for each set. Then he'd run five miles. After the roadwork the fighters would stretch as a team for almost an hour. Then training would begin. They'd spar or do pad and bag work for a few hours. Hunt then hit the gym. Pull-ups, kettlebells, deadlifts, and squats.

After training, he'd spend the morning relaxing and keeping cool in the subtropical climate. Before the sun went down, the fighters would train again for another couple of hours. After team training Hunt would have a private session with a pure boxing coach, or Jiu-Jitsu, the Brazilian version, not the one developed by the samurai, Japan's lost and wandering soldiers. In the grappling and technical aspect of Brazilian Jiu-Jitsu, which was a ground fighting style, size was of no consequence, only skill. It was about hand and arm locks and subduing an opponent on the ground while using as little effort as possible. Choke holds, elbow and joint breaks, and suffocation were key. He did nothing else. He was a specimen. Total focus on the aim.

He sucked in air and held out his gloves for the Thai

trainer to remove while he caught his breath. He went to the gym's shop, which doubled as an office, and greeted the women in the customary way, with a hands pressed together in a prayer-like stance and gave a slight bow and said, "*Sawasdee kap.*" They greeted him in return and one of the girls held out the phone.

"Hello," he said as he picked up the receiver and wiped his lip on the back of his wrapped hands.

"Mister Hunt?"

"Yes."

"It's Mandy, your Career Liaison Officer, at Royal Naval Recruiting. Sorry, sir, I've been asked to call and let you know that your application has been processed. The Command was satisfied with your board interview and medical test results and you can turn up for Royal Marine Officer Commando training."

Hunt scratched his head and closed his eyes.

"Officer? I told him -" he said in frustration. He was hot and tired and covered in sweat. His brain wasn't working as it should.

"Yes, sir."

"Ewing ..." Hunt said under his breath and pressed his palm against his forehead.

"Excuse me, sir?"

"Ah, nothing, sorry. Thanks for the call, Mandy."

"Can I tell them you'll be there?" she asked.

"Yes, ma'am. Next flight out," he said.

It was the start of a three year journey into a training regime to make him one of the elite killers on earth.

CHAPTER SEVEN

Northern Afghanistan

Three years later

Hunt sat in camouflaged fatigues at the back of a transport aircraft. The plane was bare, loud, and cold. It took sixteen hours and three refuelling stops. Hunt was the only passenger. The rest of it was fuel, food, and ammo in enormous crates to resupply the few western troops in the country. They would be alone, operating deep in enemy territory, and relying on friendly Afghan forces. For Hunt and the allied forces the only mission was: kill or capture bin Laden. Hunt was going on a manhunt in the violent and murderous countryside.

For the first time in the Special Boat Service's secretive and distinguished history most of the regiment had been deployed overseas, to conduct specialist operations in the war in Afghanistan.

On the morning of the attacks on the Twin Towers, Hunt had been in Hereford, for a combined Special Air Service and Special Boat Service exercise. The exercise had finished early and he went onto the ranges for some extra sniper training and to keep sharp. He was the only one there.

Around mid-afternoon, he heard his beeper going off in his pocket. He pulled it out and read the message. He was stunned. No-one else was around, he just said out loud to himself, "Jesus Christ! They've just attacked the United States of America ..."

His heart bled for the people who had to experience what he'd been through only three years before, instigated and planned by the same terrorist who'd taken Kelly from him.

Five days after the attack, the men of the Special Boat Service gathered to listen to the first formal post-September the eleventh briefing. Hunt had never known such a dark and focussed mood. It was a raw undercurrent of pain and anger running through the people in the briefing room. The whole regiment was assembled. Colonel Rob Saunders, the Commanding Officer, stood up to speak. A heavy silence settled over the room.

"Gentlemen, our foremost ally has been attacked, and as we speak, America is preparing her response. Make no mistake, that response will be vigorous and deadly and aimed at eliminating those responsible for the planning, financing, and executing of the attack on the World Trade Centre. As the Prime Minister made clear, the United Kingdom and her armed forces will stand with America, as America has stood with us, in this struggle against global terrorism." Colonel Rob paused and looked sternly around at his assembled troops. "After the Special Air Service have completed their operations in theatre, Director Special Forces has agreed that we will be deployed to secure Bagram airbase, which is the gateway to central Afghanistan and a highly strategic mission."

Then, on a day in early November, 'C' Squadron left the UK for the theatre of war in Afghanistan. Hunt wasn't to be one of them. 'M' and 'Z' squadrons stayed behind, on standby for counter terrorism operations in the United Kingdom. The whole world was on red alert.

LESS THAN THREE MONTHS LATER AND HUNT WAS NEEDED. He deployed on Christmas Day for a war zone. What he was needed for, he had no idea. He just sat in the back of the C-130 and tried to keep his mind clear and his body warm. At last he felt like he was going to see some action. The last few years were spent exclusively on training. Course after course. Practice after practice. From one specialist skill to the next. Like someone other than him was conducting his career. Moving pieces around the board. He often thought of the warning from the recruitment Colour Sergeant all those years ago. Before he really knew anything, especially about himself.

Over the last one thousand days his body, and his mind, had been put through the most severe stress any human can expect to be in, except for an actual war. His whole brain and being had been broken down to its bare core and then gradually, piece by piece, rebuilt in the image of, first, the Royal Marines, and then, later, the image of the Special Boat Service. The core was still there. The titanium centre. That unbreakable resolve and single mindedness remained, but what they laid on top of it should scare anyone who breached Hunt's internal and vividly-clear definition of his honour code. They put a man like him through the Royal Marine Commando course, the longest and most specialist course of its kind in the world. The specialist Cold Weather Warfare training in the Norwegian arctic. Maritime Sniper training. And then, finally, they allowed him the chance to break the back of the extreme Special Boat Service Selection course. And he did. Hunt was an Olympic level athlete. His endurance level was unsurpassed. And, more importantly, his mind was now like a bank vault. No doubt. No self-pity. His mind was now calloused and hardened against pain.

Inside, he still felt the same feeling, the feeling he'd had since the moment he realised his fiancée had died in an excruciating fireball and burned to death. The person guilty of her murder had created her death like he designed it from a blueprint. Her death was conducted, as an orchestra is conducted, in the mind and black-heart of one man. A man intelligent enough to become a surgeon. Someone with intellect who also should feel the need to heal. Instead, it was a corrupted and black type of intelligence.

The day Hunt realised that, he also knew he would see justice done for her. He knew he had to be more willing to suffer than his enemy was. So that when his life ended, and he saw her again, he could at least look her in the eyes.

What did it feel like? He'd often asked himself. In quiet moments. Hunt never dared try and explain it to anyone. He'd also never spoken about her. To anyone. Not ever. He often thought about the feeling though. It had become like another living thing inside him. Something with its own brain. Something he observed, like a child in a museum looking at a black cube behind the glass of a display cabinet. A parasitic gremlin that was alive inside him.

Ever needed a cigarette? Ever needed a cold beer on a hot day? Ever been hungry? Ever been so horny?

That feeling. Whatever that is. A need. Building, multiplying, growing inside him like an alien species. Days. Weeks. Years.

CHAPTER EIGHT

AFGHANISTAN IS a country shaped like an inkblot smudged through by a thumb. It's high above sea level and it's severely-steep mountains go up even higher. The Suleiman Mountains cut the country in half and the Hindu Kush acts as an impenetrable barrier to the north-east. The air is thin and hard to breathe. It's filled with very poor people who live in small tribal clans, and the clans have been fighting foreign invaders without pause for over two hundred years.

All of the intelligence Hunt read in preparation for his deployment showed that al-Qaeda's influence was nothing like it was in Iraq at the time, but unlike in Iraq, the Taliban and Osama bin Laden's terrorist organisation were almost interchangeable. Indeed, bin Laden and his three-thousand fanatical followers were fighting *for* the Taliban

The Taliban differed from other *mujahideen* guerrillas who'd seen off the might of the Red Army at the height of its power. They started as a student militia and morphed into fundamentalist zealots. Every one of them was schooled in *sharia* law and islamic jurisprudence in traditional Islamic schools. A *madrassa*. Internationally notorious for the most restrictive fundamentalist indoctrination.

To Hunt this made them even more dangerous than al-Qaeda. They'd fought against the Soviets. They were an angry, fanatical, sharia-following group of warrior *imams*. They carried AK-47s instead of holy books and murdered thousands upon thousands of civilians. The pace and barbarity of their assault after the Soviets left, rocked the country.

The Royal Airforce C-130 Hercules touched down with a thud. The pilot braked hard and the engines revved. Hunt was thrown sideways and caught himself on the netting. The runway was full of crater-sized potholes in the tarmac and the plane seemed to hit every one.

They'd landed about an hour north of the capital Kabul. Bagram air base, built by the Soviets, had until earlier in the month belonged to and been heavily defended by the ruling Taliban regime. It was only through the sheer force of US airstrikes and a ground assault by the friendly, indigenous, Northern Alliance troops that the strategically important runway was won.

The Kabul plateau was six-thousand feet above sea level and was surrounded by mountain ranges that went up much higher. As Hunt stepped down the back of the aircraft he saw a wild lunar landscape of breathtaking beauty. Surely it was one of the last true wildernesses on earth; but was he even still on the same planet? It was difficult to tell.

He could see his breath and the air was crisp and clear and his skin was pale from a long British winter. The sun glinted low and shone off the metal and outbuildings around him. A soldier with a thick scraggly beard and wraparound sunglasses waited at the side of a desert camouflaged British Army Land

Rover. Hunt's own beard wasn't nearly as impressive, but he'd been growing it again since before he'd found out about the deployment. It was starting to take shape.

"Hunt?" the waiting soldier said.

"That's me, yeah."

"Welcome to Bagram," the soldier said. "Baz. Welcome," Baz said again and grabbed Hunt's Bergen and lobbed it into the back of the vehicle. "You're just in time too, strike op tonight ... Come on."

They didn't have far to drive. Hunt heard the rotors of the Chinook before he saw it. The tail ramp was down and Baz drove under the spinning blades. He put the Land Rover into reverse and manoeuvred it until it was lined up with the gaping hole in the back of the chopper. Then reversed it into the transport helicopter.

CHAPTER NINE

After take off, Baz pulled out a soft pack of smokes and lit a cigarette. He held out the box. Hunt took one. Why the hell not. He was sitting in a Land Rover flying backward to wherever they were going. May as well light up.

Baz had the cigarette hanging limply out the corner of his mouth. He patted his pockets looking for a lighter. He found it in the top left breast pocket and covered the end of the cigarette as he lit it.

He held the lighter out for Hunt and yelled over the engine noise, "Mazar-i-Sharif!"

Hunt glanced at him and grinned and said, "Bless you."

"No," Baz said, "I don't have a cold, I mean, that's where we're going. Before you ask ..."

Hunt lit his cigarette and inhaled and pulled a face. As a non-smoker he always got a head rush. And said, "Thanks."

Hunt knew it. Mazar-i-Sharif meant: 'Tomb of the Prince'. The centre of the city housed an enormous and strikingly beautiful sanctuary and mosque called the 'Shrine of Ali', otherwise known as the Blue Mosque. Some Muslims believed it was the tomb of the cousin of their prophet. A holy place.

It was also the last city to fall to the fanatics after the Soviets left. It fell around the same time that Kelly was killed in the attack on the U.S. embassy. He felt a lump in his throat when he thought about her. He looked away, so Baz couldn't see his face, but Hunt doubted he would notice. Baz was too busy scratching his arse and smelling his fingers. Hunt regretted taking the lighter from him.

Mazar-i-Sharif's people opposed the Taliban. For two days after the Taliban fighters entered the city, they drove pickup trucks up and down the narrow and ancient streets and killed everything that moved—shop owners, cart pullers, women and children, even goats and donkeys. They murdered eight thousand innocent people. Their bodies lay where they fell and they filled the streets. The Taliban - the students - forbid anyone from burying the dead.

Instead, the bodies rotted in the summer heat and their flesh was eaten by packs of feral dogs. Mazar-i-Sharif was the first city won back by the U.S.-backed Northern Alliance troops.

AFTER THEY LANDED AT MAZAR INTERNATIONAL AIRPORT, Baz headed for the Special Boat Service's base.

"U.S. Military Combined Services Headquarters," Baz said and gave Hunt a sideways look of curiosity mixed with disdain. He was telling him where he was going again, before he asked. He was only a few inches short of calling Hunt a *pongo*. The Bootneck term for British Army soldiers: because their hygiene was supposedly so bad, the Royal Marines said they stank. "Old Turkish Schoolhouse," Baz said.

"What?"

"That's what it was, before it was shut down by the Talibs. No education. That's what they said, can you believe it?"

Hunt shook his head. His driver was also a tour guide and history professor.

"Don't you believe me?" Baz asked.

"No, I believe you," Hunt said.

The schoolhouse turned out to be a squat three-storey building. The top floor was the Central Intelligence Agency and U.S. Army Special Forces Operational Detachment – Delta; better known as Delta Force. Middle floor housed the U.S. 5th Special Forces Group and a detachment of Rangers. And, on the bottom, the 10th Mountain Division, reputed to have the U.S. Army's toughest soldiers.

The Special Boat Service guys seemed to float amongst them all, brought in to help wherever their specialist skills could be put to best use to achieve a tactical advantage. Given the freedom to float, Hunt preferred to be on the top floor, closest to the strategic picture. He wanted to better understand the complexity of this chess match of grand strategy.

CHAPTER TEN

US Military Combined Services Headquarters, Mazar-i-Sharif

AFTER HE'D BEEN THERE for some time, Hunt inserted himself into the Delta operations room. Hunt made himself useful by gathering signals intelligence from the Taliban's ICOM radio communications. He had a headset on and listened to chatter over the Japanese-built ICOM radios the insurgents used.

His rudimentary Pashto rapidly improved. He started to recognise the speakers' voices and pictured where they were in his mind's-eye, in relation to the messages and sounds in the background of their conversations.

Often, the enemy would give a running commentary on the troop movements they were observing, or what the foreign forces were doing. Whether buying chickens in the *bazaar* or nearly stepping on homemade bombs they'd planted.

The door to the mini-ops room banged open. Hunt turned from the desk and his notepad fell on the floor. One the Central Intelligence Agency guys walked in. It sounded like it might get fiery. Tensions had been high and everyone was worried about a Taliban counter attack to retake the strategically important city they were currently in.

The CIA guy was in his mid-fifties, a little overweight. His belly hung over the front of his jeans and squeezed out the sides of a black polo shirt. He had a short, fair-haired moustache that twitched as he spoke.

"Dalton!" he called out as he walked into the room.

He was followed in by a uniformed commander in the guerrilla combat shirt and green beret of the French Foreign Legion. The beret puffed like a meringue and looked as if it might fall off any moment. Behind the duo was a taller, thinner, pale-skinned guy. He was youngish, or maybe he just had boyish looks, Hunt couldn't tell. It was probably the swept over British public schoolboy brown hair that gave it away. Hunt hadn't seen him before, but since he'd walked in, the schoolboy hadn't taken his eyes off Hunt. It felt odd. The CIA guy was looking for the Delta Force commander, James Dalton, and called out his name again. Dalton hung up his phone call and stood up. He puffed his cheeks and pulled up his combat trousers at the belt.

"Dalton," the CIA guy said when he saw the commander. "We need one of your snipers."

"I'm well, how you doin'?" Dalton said.

He was short, stocky, with a shaved head and serious face. He'd been in Tora Bora and knew what the hell was going on. He walked out from behind the ops desks and met the visitors in the middle of the room. The comment went over the

CIA green-slime's head. Pond life. That's what intelligence guys were thought of as.

"This is Colonel Harvey Wallenbland," the intelligence guy said and gestured to the Foreign Legion commander without introducing Dalton to him. The French colonel raised his hand and opened his mouth to speak, he looked as if he was about to correct the CIA guy's pronunciation of his name, but Dalton cut him off.

"No guys spare I'm afraid, all are otherwise engaged," Dalton said.

The CIA guy flicked his head at the Frenchman, "Their sniper is dead. This morning. Took a mortar round in the teeth," the CIA guy said. "The Legion are supporting our ops in the mountains to protect the city and they *need* one of your snipers ..."

"Not my problem," Dalton said. "Hell, if it's in the mountains go'n ask the tenth guys in the basement."

Dalton pulled a face that said, 'sorry, wish I could help' and shrugged. As far as he was concerned the conversation was over and he turned to leave.

"We checked already. They have a guy, five kills, but he is at least two days away," the CIA guy said.

Dalton stopped in his tracks. Hunt took the headset off and stood up. No-one paid him any attention, except the tall schoolboy-looking one who was standing quietly at the back like a diligent swot. Hunt raised his hand and the schoolboy stepped forward suddenly and walked towards him.

"Captain Hunt, Special Boat Service, isn't it?" he said and stuck out his hand as he strode over. Hunt shook the outstretched hand coming at him with the extraterrestrial-length fingers. Hunt'd never seen this man in his life, yet this guy knew his name and his unit. The schoolboy turned to the rest of the men standing there.

"You're a sniper, aren't you, Hunt?"

Hunt pulled out of the handshake. Everyone looked at him.

"Well, aren't you?" the tall-schoolboy said again.

"Yes, sir," Hunt said looking at Dalton. "Marine sniper."

The other three men looked him up and down.

"Oh, yeah," the CIA guy said. "How many kills?"

"Two," the tall-schoolboy said and held up two fingers. He lied. Hunt had none, but Stirling didn't correct him, he wanted to go on the operation.

"What're you, British?" the CIA guy asked and sideways-glanced at the Legionnaire, as if that might be a problem for the Frenchman.

"Yeah," Hunt said. "Is that an issue? We're all in this together, aren't we?"

"Well, *parlez-vous Français?*" Dalton asked him with a wry smile.

Hunt shrugged. He spoke a bit.

"Well, I guess, you're it," the CIA guy said. "Deploy tonight."

The tall-schoolboy grinned at Hunt. If that was rehearsed, it went off better than opening night.

"Thomas Holland, Her Majesty's Secret Intelligence, at your service," the tall man said and stuck his hand out. This time, Hunt shook lightly and slowly. He looked at Holland a bit sideways. He was unsure about what had just happened.

CHAPTER ELEVEN

THE MISSION BRIEFING was in French and a lot of it went over Hunt's head. Occasionally he would hear *Capitaine 'Aunt* and knew they were talking about him, or his part of the mission, and he perked up.

The chatter was that Dadullah Akhund, the Taliban commander, better known as Mullah Dadullah, was headed back to Mazar-i-Sharif to lead the recapture of the important northern city.

Though he had a funny sounding name, while still a young man, Mullah Dadullah lost a leg in the fight against Soviet occupation in the eighties. He had also overseen the slaughter of the Persian-speaking peoples in central Afghanistan. He was one of the ten leaders of the Taliban and a fierce and brutal man. At least making a positive identification would be easy. Hunt had to look out for a guy hopping around on one leg. That, and his trademark tightly wrapped, pitch-black turban.

Rumours had reached the ears of the CIA that over eight thousand Taliban fighters would descend from the mountains to the south of Mazar-i-Sharif. In turn, over a thousand US

Army Rangers were airlifted into the city as protection. This was real Roman-siege style warfare.

Hunt's mission was to infiltrate a mountainous range to the south-east of the Kuh-e Mogholan mountain on the border between Baglan and Tachar provinces. The target village was called Yawur and they were to report back any intelligence on troop movements or suspicious activity. Yawur meant 'tied up', so named because the valley below the mountain range was knotted and dense like a noose. It tightened as you pulled on it. It was an area where a small cluster of villages intersected. Hunt would need to get into an overwatch position above one of those villages and find Dadullah. He and his spotter were allocated the southernmost village.

Hunt was paired with a spotter from the French Foreign Legion named Philipe Lambert. He had an English mother and French father and the romance of the Legion had lured him in. He had bright eyes, brown hair, and a very personable manner. Too enthusiastic and comical for war. He spoke good English. It was his first combat mission in Afghanistan. He was the radio operator. Hunt was the medic and sniper.

Hunt and Lambert were to be one of four, two-man teams, choppered into the low ground at the base of the mountain range. Then they would climb up through the mountain pass and into an overwatch position. The positions had been surveyed by satellite and they had a ten digit grid that pinpointed each location overlooking one of the four exits of the target villages.

Two Black Hawk helicopters and two Apache gunships would fly under the cover of darkness. Each two man team would then fast rope to the ground in their own area of operations and begin the long, arduous march up the hills. Hills turned into mountains. Mountains turned into the ranges that rose up out of the centre of the country like a crown of thorns.

While the other Chinook made ghost drops as a decoy to confuse any enemy that might be on the ground, Hunt and Lambert fast-roped down and inserted themselves on a saddle ridge between the biggest mountain in the area called Kuh-e Mogholan, which meant Mongol Mountain. The target mountain ridge was called Chashmeh-ye Rabat. Source of Glass. Hunt wondered if that was because of the sheer sides and slippery-smooth cliffs.

Hunt hit the dusty-shale surface and dipped his head in a crouch. The powerful downdraft pushed down on them. As the helicopter ascended, the pressure lifted. It flew off into the blackness. They found cover and waited. They stayed still. They regained their calm. Once they were accustomed to the night, the noises, and the sounds, they moved out.

Each man carried a Bergen with rations, ammunition, water, and their personal ghillie suits. Their sniper suits were camouflaged with the colours of the environment and had no discernible outline or pattern. Each man had made his own during sniper training. And each man had modified theirs for the environment they were operating in.

There was no silhouette to break them up from the colours and textures of their backdrop. The first ever sniper unit was recruited from Scottish highland game keepers and professional stalkers during the First World War. The name ghillie suit came from the name of an earth spirit from Scottish mythology which was clothed in leaves and moss.

Hunt and Lambert moved like spirits now, through the silent barren landscape, as they glided up and up the sheer slopes.

They contoured along the spine of a ridge that ran to the top of the mountain pass. Hunt and Lambert arrived at the pass sometime before dawn. They both stopped for a moment to observe the very early morning light on the horizon. They gave each other a look and Hunt nodded and they proceeded forward in silence.

They were descending down into one of the veins of the valley that connected into the main artery which ran eastwards towards Peshawar, the biggest majority-Pashtun city, which was just over the border in the country of Pakistan. Hunt knew some of the history of this region. It was a similar problem to the random carving up of land in British Colonial Africa which led to so much conflict between different tribes.

Hunt imagined the history as if it was happening now. It was more real to him being in the very place it had happened. He walked, slow and silent, downhill, in the darkness. His knees took the brunt of the weight of the pack and his thighs burned as they resisted against gravity and the steep decline. His boots slipped and skidded on the loose rock.

The Amir back then was a man weak in power and not in control of his own country. This was the man that submitted to British demands and partitioned his country down the middle of the Sulaiman Mountains. This created a border with the British Raj, which was the whole of the Indian subcontinent, at that time.

The new border cleaved a proud people in half. It put a demarcation line between the capital city of the Pashtun people, and the rest of their extended families and tribes that lived further to the west, past the mountainous new border, in the east and south of Afghanistan. These were the same places where the Taliban originated. From the same tribe that had been fighting for an independent Pashtun state for over two hundred years.

Hunt and Lambert had just climbed over the exact point where the tectonic plates of Eurasia and India collided over thirty-million years ago and formed the fold and thrust mountain chain separating Europe from Asia. It was a border of peoples, countries, continents, and it festered with conflict.

As they descended, the foliage started to thicken. At first it was spiky and tough-looking shrubbery. As they dropped in altitude and further into the tree line, it grew thicker and wilder with forests. Hunt looked up at the swaying and cracking branches as they floated eerily above them. The trees must've been hundreds of years old. Undisturbed for all this time. It was like stepping back in time.

Hunt's feelings made him realise why ancient people believed evil spirits lived in the woods. At night it was a place of extreme danger. Even with night vision they moved blindly. Only the piercingly high frequency whine of the goggles broke the silence and turned the blackness around them into different shades of throbbing green radiation, like some toxic vision of a post-nuclear world.

They moved slower now. Layers upon layers of twigs and needles from the giant fir trees overhead littered the floor. It was impossible to walk without sound. Each step made a crunch and snap. Each time Hunt placed his foot down the sound was amplified like a gunshot in his head. He knew the fear was a good thing.

Anxiousness and fear came from the same place. His adrenal system. The difference was that the intensity of the training he'd been exposed to meant that he continued to move forward. His mind was trained to react to anxiety by putting the fighting skills he'd learned to work. It was automatic. No rest, no sleep, no food, no excuses, and then the

Special Boat Service would do close quarter battle drills using living people as hostages and live rounds. So, Hunt concentrated on moving forward.

Still before dawn the pair identified and agreed on a safe-looking location they could use as a final rendezvous and fall back point and store their kit and equipment. It was set back from the rocky cliff face that overlooked the valley. It had a horseshoe shape of boulders protecting it from three sides. It faced the cliff and valley below them.

They squared themselves away and protected the hide. And settled into their concealed position. It was bitterly cold. Hunt's sweat dried as his body cooled. It had been a hard trek. He wrapped up and climbed into his sleeping bag with his L118A1 Arctic Warfare 50 (AW50) sniper rifle resting on his chest.

It had a heavy, long, match-grade, free-floating steel barrel and was capable of ultra-high distance kills. The rest of the frame was made from aluminium and it weighed around twenty-five pounds. It was specifically designed to be used in freezing conditions. It was an elite weapon in the right hands.

It was fitted with a L17A1 Schmidt & Bender MK II 50mm scope, which had a kill-flash screwed onto the front of the variable 3-12 zoom sight. It prevented light from reflecting off the glass and metal and giving his position away. The scope also had a single picatinny rail on top onto which Hunt could attach an image intensifying night scope. He could attach a SIMRAD night vision on top of the scope and see the intensified image through the Schmidt & Bender scope aperture. It turned the ten-round NATO-standard 7.62 sniper rifle into something that resembled a piece of optical equipment with a barrel attached. It also had an offset, attachable, picatinny rail which was used to hold a Sniper Thermal Imaging Capability (STIC) scope in place. At night, at a distance, Hunt would be able to see the orange glow of heat being emitted from enemy bodies. No-one was going to be able to sneak around in the dark. They had nowhere to hide. Overall, it was a formidable long range weapon unique to the British Special Forces.

The pair made a stag roster for the short time they might have to sleep. They needn't have bothered. They stayed awake and simply remained silent in the darkness. Hunt tried not to let his mind amplify the sounds that surrounded them this deep into enemy territory.

Once they were settled into the final rendezvous and fall back position, Lambert tried to raise the headquarters and give them another SITREP. All he got back was static. He tried again and again, but no joy. They weren't concerned though.

After first light they would conceal their equipment, find a radio signal, confirm their position with the ops room, and proceed to finding a suitable position to provide overwatch.

THEY 'STOOD TO' BEFORE FIRST LIGHT. A STANDARD operating procedure. Every morning and every night whether on exercise or operations, soldiers were to 'stand to' from half an hour before first light, until half an hour after first light. The same at last light. Each man would stand to around their own *basha*, or shelter. The reason for it was that those were the two most likely times for an enemy to attack, and the two times that friendly forces were most likely to be tired and lethargic. And the enemy knew it. It was a tense period of time.

The light from the sunrise came up directly over the steep-sided valley in front of them. It hit them straight in the eyes and the high-up forest transitioned from nocturnal rhythms to diurnal ones as it warmed and the daylight woke the animals. Hunt and Lambert concealed their Bergens and covered the area over with a camouflaged *basha* and loose sticks and leaves. Hunt signalled to Lambert that they should move forward to the edge of the trees. The two men made their way forward. It was tactical and slow movement. They stopped just inside the line of trees. With his naked eye, Hunt could see white smoke rising from mud-walled houses in the valley below. The sun bounced off the white earth and gave it a dazzling yellow shimmer. He took out his combat binoculars. While Hunt observed the target and assessed the best spot for concealment with maximum visibility, Lambert tried for comms. He repeatedly sent radio checks out on different settings and with different sized antennas. Hunt glanced back at him and Lambert shook his head. They had no option but to proceed with their mission and try for comms later in the day, perhaps from a different, more exposed location. They were in danger of missing two communications windows and that would be cause for the ops room to get concerned.

CHAPTER TWELVE

Lambert came forward to join Hunt on the rocky outcrop overlooking the village. The sun was up now and moved to their right, low over the horizon. They were both in ghillie suits, full black cam cream, and with indigenous shrubbery fixed to their hessian covers. It was still cold, but the layers of camouflage kept them warm. Hunt looked out from the overwatch position he'd chosen.

The mountains in the distance seemed to go on and on until the white capped peaks were lost in a haze. Hunt used his rifle scope to survey the village below. It was purely reconnaissance.

"Still nothing on the radio?" Hunt asked as he looked through the sight with one eye closed. Lambert lay on his belly and held a spotting scope to his eye and followed Hunt's view. "It isn't just your budget cheese-eating-surrender-monkey equipment?" Hunt asked with his tongue firmly in his cheek.

"We know there is nothing wrong with the equipment," Lambert said, with the seriousness of a Frenchman. "We got through on the waypoints on the climb. I reach not even the other sniper teams."

"Interference from the mountain?"

Lambert silently shrugged.

"You can see the whole goddamn village from up here," Hunt said as he put the red chevron from the sight on the villagers below. There was a lot of activity for a small village. And, it was only men. When the Taliban were in charge they forbade women from leaving their homes.

"That's not just a few villagers down there," Hunt said.

"It's a whole *putain de* army," Lambert said.

He was right. Hunt and Lambert were looking at a concentration of Taliban and al-Qaeda like nothing the allied forces in Afghanistan had ever encountered.

The estimate for the number of al-Qaeda fighters in the Tora Bora caves was a few hundred. Hunt could be looking at a few thousand fighters in this, and the other nearby villages. The reports were true. They had to warn the others, and they had to do it now. Mazar-i-Sharif was in danger.

"*Merde*," Lambert said as he crawled backwards and stood to climb back up to the cliff face and into the tree line. "I need to arrange the comms."

"No shit. Get it sorted ..." Hunt said as Lambert pulled out his gear inside the tree line. They were over nine-hundred meters away from the target village, around three-thousand feet. Well within range for Hunt's sniper rifle, but they still had to call it in and get authorisation to make any kills. They could only do that after they'd identified Mullah Dadullah.

HUNT WAS ALONE ON THE FLAT-TOPPED OUTCROP OF ROCKS. He kept on looking at the village through his rifle sight. He had a waterproof notepad and pencil next to the rifle, and with it he drew schematics of the village. In the near distance, closer to his position and south of the village, a farmer was in his fields with his son. He sat on top of a red tractor and the boy stood in the field at the front. He was trying to pull something or move something from a ditch. Hunt could see, but not hear the low growl of the engine and the clanking of metal as the machine's massive rear tyres tried to reverse and pull out a stump. The farmer had a front bucket claw attachment to the tractor. He'd tied a rope to the front and the machine was trying desperately to move the obstacle. The rope strained. Hunt could feel the tension. Something was going to give. *Snap*. The rope broke and Hunt smiled at the wholesome scene and then moved the magnified image north, back onto the village.

He included approximate distances between walls, their heights, and any obstacles or obstructions which might make it difficult for a bigger force to destroy the target. Hunt also made notes on the different people he saw as they moved around the village. They were predominantly fighting-aged males, but Hunt could see that there were different groups and different ethnicities. Some of the combatants were taller and thinner, they looked proud, with straight noises and lighter coloured skin. Hunt thought it likely that these men were Saudi Arabian, like bin Laden. Others were shorter with a much darker complexion. They didn't have beards. Hunt assessed these men to be, more than likely, from nearby Pakistan. It was clear to him that the fighting force in the village were Taliban and predominantly Pashtuns. They had even paler skin overall, some of the tribes even had red hair and blue eyes.

Hunt knew that up in the north of the country, in the mountain fastness of Nuristan the tribes were fair-haired with blue-eyes, and freckles. Very different to anyone else in these mountains and valleys.

It could be possible that that race of blonde-haired, blue-eyed people moved, slowly over centuries, from high-up in the Hindu Kush, all the way down to the Baltic Sea and spawned the Vikings. There was no doubt that the people of this mountainous and brutal country were, first and foremost, tribes of warriors. Hunt thought that what he was looking at could be assessed as a village filled with al-Qaeda fighters. They were a fanatical warrior tribe of a different kind ... followers of an ideology that needed to be scrubbed from the face of the planet; just as they wanted - were commanded - to scrub non-believers from the face of the planet.

Hunt stayed in the same place all day. He took many notes and observed as many people as he could. He lay on his stomach and rested on his elbows for almost seven hours without a break to even take a leak. He started to fade. His concentration was slipping. He rubbed his eyes. Just a few more hours to hold on.

He knew that, come sunset, the village would again grow quiet. He would stay to see what the general movement pattern in the evening was. Hunt was observing one particular house near the middle of the village that seemed to have an above normal level of activity. People had been coming and going all day and Hunt saw the pale-blue metal gate to the compound open and close continuously. Then, while he watched with the red chevron right on the entrance, a few younger boys and younger men came out of the compound.

Hunt watched. He saw the younger boys make a gap and a hole opened in the assembled crowd. He had clear visibility of the front gate. Hunt first saw the white beard and the white turban and then did a double take. His mind immediately went into overdrive. His pupils dilated and his heart rate increased. He was totally alert and focussed now. The level of adrenaline in his body was through the roof. He'd just seen Ayman al-Zawahiri. He was sure of it. Could he be sure? Yes.

It was him. In the flesh. Behind the man he thought was al-Zawahiri, another man with his weight on one crutch, wearing a black turban, followed him out. But Hunt didn't care. He only had eyes for al-Zawahiri.

Hunt watched. He couldn't take his eyes off him. He'd never seen him this close up before. He studied the face. The lines on it. The glasses he wore. The way he smiled and patted the young children on the head. Hunt's mission had changed. This was al-Zawahiri. This was al-Qaeda's number two. This was the man who murdered his fiancée. Nothing else mattered. Hunt and Lambert had managed to positively identify al-Zawahiri and Dadulla at the same time, on the same day. He knew this could be a once in a lifetime opportunity.

They needed to tell the headquarters as soon as possible, and get the quick reaction force and an AC-130 Spectre gunship on target. The Angel of Death could come and point its heavily armed weapons systems at this village and flatten it. He'd happily pick through the wreckage and identify al-Zawahiri's body, and then put a 9mm round in the skull just to be sure. A snatch and grab, or butcher and bold mission. Either would work.

For Hunt, preferably the latter. It had to happen. Unconsciously, Hunt turned the safety off the AW50. And then, consciously, worked the bolt. He put a round in the chamber and never took his eyes off his target. The tip of the red chevron came to rest on the bridge of al-Zawahiri's nose. Hunt inhaled, and held his diaphragm, before gently exhaling.

As he inhaled the red chevron raised and as he exhaled it lowered until the tip of the red pyramid rested, and was still, on his target's left ear. He held his breath.

Hunt applied some light pressure to the trigger. And breathed again. It would be a short flight for the bullet and it would be an angle from high to low with gravity doing its work and the bullet descending the whole way. There was very little wind and what there was came from behind Hunt's position. There were no clouds. The bullet would spin out of the barrel at eight hundred and twenty-five meters per second. It would take just over one second to arc downward on the wind, along the length of the valley, and smack right into the centre of al-Zawahiri's face. Hunt could see the spray of pink mist blasting out of the back of al-Zawahiri's head in his mind's-eye.

Al-Zawahiri ducked now to hug some children that had gathered around him. He had a smile on his face, but Hunt could see the deadness and blackness behind his eyes. He seemed jovial and the men chatted and laughed. It was like a meet and greet. Hunt kept the chevron following al-Zawahiri's turbaned head.

What had they just been discussing? Had they just had a *shura* to consult on the plan to retake the city of Mazar-i-Sharif ... and about what they were going to do to all the women and children in the city, once they recaptured it? Had they discussed rape and murder? Just to show the people who was in control. Who was in charge. That no one was more powerful than *Allah*.

Hunt knew he had to suppress his emotions. In the time he had his finger applying pressure to the trigger, the left side of his brain managed to fight through the descending cloud of revenge and consider the risks. The biggest risk was that he was about to undermine the wider operation. Did it matter though? It was al-Zawahiri. He might be about to put all of the other snipers overlooking the valley in danger. Did he care about that? No. Their lives were worth sacrificing if it meant taking the life of the man who killed the love of his life.

He knew the exact amount of tension the trigger needed. How firmly he could depress it until the mechanism activated. It was right on the limit.

A gust of wind might force it, engage the hammer, and send a single round into the valley below.

CHAPTER THIRTEEN

Just then a bigger group came out of the compound door and surrounded al-Zawahiri and Dadulla. Hunt released the tension in the trigger and swallowed hard and breathed again. He couldn't take his eyes off the white turban. He knew the moment was gone. He still wasn't thinking straight.

He tried to calm down. He tried to think clearly about what needed to be done. But, all of his thoughts and emotions and deepest darkest desires were getting out, like demons from hell.

Despite all the training he'd endured to stamp these emotions out, Hunt couldn't see anything besides Kelly's face imploring him, with tears in her eyes, to remove this evil from the planet. Hunt wanted to turn him into a scatter of unidentifiable organic matter. He wanted this person to become fertiliser.

He'd seen enough. It was nearly dusk. The village was free of movement. Hunt started to collapse his position and moved back into the tree line. As he was about to, he caught the *buzz* of a Japanese scooter being carried on the wind. He decided to check.

"Well, what do we have here," he said to himself. A youth, with a wispy moustache and wearing a traditional Afghan cap over his thick black hair drove the scooter while an older, bearded man in a turban held on behind him. They came riding out to the south of the village. They pulled over at a narrow point of a dry irrigation ditch, or *wadi*. The youth got down on his hands and knees and started digging. He pushed the mud up the shallow bank and made a divot.

"What the ... bastards," Hunt said. His blood was up. He wanted to blast them away. The older man climbed into the freshly dug trough and started to bury an unexploded munitions shell. All Hunt could do was note the approximate grid reference on his map. He kept watching. Hunt was both horrified and impressed by their total disregard for their own safety. There they were, so confident in the rusted, homemade explosive device that neither of them had any protective equipment at all. Standard operating procedure in Afghanistan was *Insha'Allah*. God's will. They covered over the device and Hunt watched as the old man carefully placed the wired pressure pad on top of the path next to the irrigation ditch. The youth took some stones from his pocket and made a small mound next to where they'd laid the bomb. It was to be a warning for anyone walking nearby ... if they were lucky enough to see it. When the job was complete they started the scooter and drove back to the village.

Hunt packed up his gear and moved in a crouch with his rifle in his shoulder. He pivoted around the centre of his gravity, just in case he stumbled upon the enemy, or they stumbled upon him. There was no rest. He found Lambert still fighting with the radios.

"Bastards were laying an IED next to the *wadi* ..." Hunt said. It was a bit absentminded. "Just now. Didn't even wait 'til dark. Can you believe it?"

"It's no *bloody* use ..." Lambert said. "I can't get this *bloody* thing to do its *bloody* job ..."

Hunt only half listened to him. He was still away with the demons. The sun was setting and he felt the chill under the canopy of fir trees. Hunt crouched down next to Lambert in the shelter.

"Listen," Hunt said, "There's something I need to tell you ..." His eyes were wide and Lambert stopped what he was doing and looked at him. "I saw him. I saw our target, Mullah Dadulla, down in the village just now ... I also think they're al-Qaeda, not just Taliban."

"What makes you say that?"

Hunt shook his head, "Their dress, the way they look, I also saw someone that looked like al-Zawahiri."

"Who?"

"Who!" Hunt said. He was incredulous and still fuming about the missed chance to kill him. "No one. He's just a top, top guy in al-Qaeda ..." Hunt answered. "No big deal ... Except, I'm sure our friends back in Mazar would be a bit interested."

"No need to be such a little bitch." Lambert said. "So, we need to find a way to let them know?"

"Preferably," Hunt said. He was losing patience. If he'd had any to begin with.

"It's nearly last light," Lambert said. "We can't do anything about this tonight ... Can we?"

A perfect French attitude. Leave it until tomorrow. "No," Hunt said, "But, by the morning it may be too late. These are the guys who brought an army of foreign fighters back to within spitting distance of a city where they've already slaughtered the population once, just for defending themselves. We can't let that happen again."

Lambert nodded pensively. Hunt admired his calmness. "No, but what can we do? Do you want us to trace our steps back to the mountain, at night, to where we can get comms?"

"We might have to ... unless you get your shit sorted and stop making us look like amateurs," Hunt said.

Lambert smiled at first and then realised Hunt wasn't joking. And he sulked.

***

Lambert sat with his back leaning up against the rocks that formed the amphitheatre-like protective area. He had a sketch pad on his lap and the rough drawings that Hunt had done. The Englishman rolled over and handed him a steaming hot steel flask lid of coffee.

"*Merci*," Lambert said and placed it next to him. He saw Captain Hunt peering at his work.

"Can I see?" Hunt asked.

Lambert held the sketch so that he could see. Hunt looked at him with a surprised look, like he was about to say, 'did you draw that?'

"I used to be an artist," Lambert said. The Englishman looked impressed.

"That is very impressive," Hunt said. "Makes my drawings look like Billy aged five. Yours are so realistic. I mean, to be able to do that with no sleep on the side of a mountain is ... So, if you were an artist, what made you join the Legion?"

"Well, not an artist. More like a forger. I tried to sell some forgeries and got caught. It was stupid. So, I stopped doing that. Then I broke into some important looking homes and stole their art. I was young and naive and stupid," Lambert said and used the edge of the pencil to shade one side of the mosque from the village below them. He couldn't see it of course, he only had the image in his head to sketch from, and Hunt's scribbles.

"Yeah," Hunt said. Lambert thought he was contemplating the meaning of the choices we make. But then again, he was a 'roast beef' and who knows the depths of their minds. Certainly not as creative and artistic as a Frenchman. He smiled at his own insolence.

"You know much about the art world?" Lambert asked.

Hunt looked away and shook his head then back at Lambert, "Not much, no."

"It's where rich people hide their money. A closed market. I have thought a lot about art. It is a commodity with no inherent value. Only something that has value because of scarcity and because rich people want a place to hide their money. It only has value when someone else can buy it. Which is why art thievery is not lucrative, even if the paintings themselves are worth millions. The buyer cannot market the piece, unless it is for his own personal collection."

"What happened then?" Hunt asked him and took a sip of his coffee.

"I was given a choice by the Judge. Either, join the Legion and straighten myself out, or go to prison for five years. I chose five years in the Legion. It was the best decision I ever made," he said with a smile on his face.

Hunt looked around at their meagre camp and gestured around the thin forest around them. "Yeah, I mean, what could be better, what more could we want," he said sarcastically and Lambert nodded in appreciation. He was happy that they shared the same sense of humour. *L'humeur macabre*. Gallows humour. The soldier's staple around the world. The proximity to death, and fear of injury, made jokes about coming home in a coffin, or missing a limb, a potency in the same way as a bullet hissing over your head gave you a visceral appreciation for breath and colours.

"Do you know about rock bottom?" he asked the Englishman.

"A thing or two."

"Then you know why I joined the Legion."

Lambert saw the Englishman nod as the light faded.

They 'stood to' from half an hour before last light. Hunt had plenty of time to think as the sun ducked behind the mountains and its warmth gave way to the angry cold. The bird song gave way to the incessant howling and barking from dogs far below them in the village. Afghans, behind their compounds of high-walled mud homes, were notorious for the size and ferocity of their dogs. This was a country where bull baiting and dog fighting were still two of the main pastimes.

To get a dog to fight for you, and put its life on the line for you, it really has to love you. And, you have to at least love what it is willing to do for you, for a dog to trust you enough that it will fight another dog. Fighting isn't a natural state for dogs. Just like it isn't a natural state for human beings. It takes a uniquely evil person to kill innocence, and it takes a uniquely honourable person to kill evil people on behalf of those who can't protect themselves. After it was dark and they'd been lying silently for an hour, they got up, and collapsed back to their position of safety. Hunt started sorting through his gear.

"What are you doing?" Lambert asked, as he opened a cold ration pack and diligently dipped his racing spoon into the greasy gravy-covered meatballs.

"I'm going to leave my gear here ..." Hunt said. Lambert looked up at him with the spoon in his mouth and sat motionless. Hunt saw from the look he could make out on his face and his silence that he was concerned. "You go back to the north-west face and get comms. I'm going down to the village to try and get a closer look at the ground."

"What? Do you want to go down into the village?" Lambert asked.

"I want to make sure it is who I think it is ... Don't worry, I'm not going to get caught."

"I don't think that's a good idea," Lambert said. "I think we both go back together to the other side and try and get comms."

Hunt said, "What if they leave? Or, what if they mobilise and depart, and we lose them?"

"There are other snipers, other teams, they will see them ..."

"We don't know that ..." Hunt said. "And, frankly, that isn't the way we do things. Where I'm from, we get the job done. Understand? We can't let these guys escape. And, if you can get comms you can talk them onto the position, and let them know what we've seen." Hunt handed Lambert the waterproof notepad with his sketches and human intelligence gathering. "It's also got schematics of the village in there," Hunt said and pointed to the notebook in Lambert's hands.

Lambert looked down at the notebook, but didn't say anything. Hunt could feel that he wasn't convinced.

"This is the plan," Hunt said, "You wait until first light then go back to the last checkpoint, where we had comms. We've missed two windows anyway, so they're bound to be worried. We can't have them compromise the mission just because they think we're in danger. Once you get comms up, you come back to this overwatch position here and let me know that you were successful."

"How?"

"Try my PRC. If that doesn't work, use your mirror and flash a blink of sunlight at the village. I'll be looking for it."

Lambert shook his head and dipped the spoon into the foil bag of meatballs. "And what about you?" he asked with his mouth full.

"I'll blend in," Hunt said, and tried to sound like he had a plan. "I'll go down and make sure they don't leave. And, if they do try to, I'll make sure they don't. Let's swap weapons. You take the sniper and I'll take the Minimi."

Lambert shrugged. "You're the ranking officer," he said. "But, just tell me one thing. Do you have a death wish?"

Hunt said nothing. They sat silently in the dark for a moment and Hunt heard the metal spoon go back into the aluminium ration bag and Lambert put a mouthful of goop and he slurped a bit. "Because," he said finally, mouth full of oily-tomatoey bile, "I will tell them not to risk their lives coming to look for you. If you have a death wish ..."

Hunt didn't know what to say, so he said nothing. It sounded fair.

"*Anglais fou*," Lambert said quietly to himself. "What're you try to be, some kind of English Assassin? *Imbécile*."

Lambert wasn't impressed. Hunt didn't blame him. Then again, it wasn't Hunt whose comms equipment or bad drills put him in the position to have to make this decision. There are no easy decisions in war, only lucky ones, and generally, Hunt felt, fortune favoured the brave. He left Lambert to eat his gruel.

CHAPTER FOURTEEN

Hunt waited until after midnight. He and Lambert hadn't slept. Hunt silently lifted his webbing and slung it, picked up his new rifle, and checked his holster and sidearm. His new rifle was the M249 SAW Paratrooper version of the FN Minimi. A 5.56 millimetre light machine gun that Lambert had carried. SAW stood for Squad Automatic Weapon.

It had a collapsible stock and was a gas operated, air-cooled, automatic rifle. It was shorter and considerably lighter than the regular M249, but with the same suppressing power.

Hunt had taken all of the thirty-round NATO-magazines when he packed his kit, thinking he was definitely going to need them. Better to be prepared for war than not. They'd decided to use standard magazines instead of the more cumbersome and noisier boxes of linked ammunition. If it came to it, they were going to put down hundreds of rounds of covering fire, they would be beating a veracious tactical retreat and the Minimi would be aimed and deadly.

Hunt slung the weapon over his shoulder and checked the

magazine was secure in the side of the machine gun. He pulled the charging handle and released it and it slammed forward. The weapon was loaded. He put it in safe with his thumb.

"Don't get killed," Lambert said as he readied himself.

"Cheers, pal," Hunt said.

Lambert would take the sniper rifle onto the ledge with the thermal imaging sight attached and watch Hunt's descent into hell.

Hunt left their position and made his way to the rocky ridge that led down into the valley and the narrow gap of an entrance to the village. It was a clear night and the moon hung low in a sky filled with stars. It looked like he could just reach up and pluck one from the night air, like a rose from a bush. He didn't really even need the night vision goggles. Often he preferred to operate at night without them, and not have the high pitched whine in his ears, but of all the nights, this was the most prudent to use them.

Even though it was clear, it was still slow going. It was loose underfoot and he would slip and stones would roll down the sharp sides of the ridge and fall into the trees and rocky outcrops of the valley below.

Hunt tried not to think about tumbling down there himself. It took him around two hours to descend to the base. Once at the bottom of the ridge he found a tributary, a small stream, which led into the bigger Darya-e-Bangi river, which flowed south to north. He knelt and removed his gloves and washed his hands and his face and neck. It was freezing cold. Hunt took on some water from his webbing and then continued on.

He did have a plan. It was a loose sort of plan right now, and would require improvisation, something the military weren't great at, but it ended with the assassination of the

Doctor of Death, Ayman al-Zawahiri. And, hopefully not his own.

During his reconnaissance and intelligence gathering from the ledge, Hunt had noticed a family-sized mud house, inside a compound wall. There was a farmer's smallholding field outside the gate and Hunt had seen him tending to it.

The farmer and his family were on the south-westerly approach to the village. The compound was isolated, and secluded, and the wall was only high enough that, in the worst case, he might have to slide over it. The first stage of his plan was to find the washing line and commandeer a traditional Pashtun outfit.

He was sure, based on his experience blending in during the escape and evasion phase of selection, and his experience in Cairo before, that he had the ability to disguise himself and fit in. Hunt had seen so many different nationalities, and types of people in the village, that he would be able to be like a mosquito on the wall. Annoying and difficult to identify.

One of the things Hunt had read in preparation for his deployment was Mountstuart Elphinstone's account of his mission back in the early nineteenth century. The book told tales of the resilience and hospitality of the Afghan people, but above all, it told of an honour code called the *pashtunwali* that all Pashtuns lived by. It dictated that Afghans must be ruthless enemies, but it also made them duty bound to risk their own lives to guarantee the safety of their guests.

It was a balance of extremes that maintained a bizarre equilibrium for centuries. It was an honour code that preceded the Taliban by a thousand years and would be there a thousand years after they left. It was as in-built into their biology and harder to break than the stone in the mountains surrounding them. Its rules set behaviours which ensured eternal blood feuds and infinite friendships.

The code of honour was upheld by an Afghan people of charm and grace, who'd amassed elaborate codes of dress, and were capable of the most caring hospitality, alongside the most unfathomable cruelty. *Pashtunwali* demanded respect for Imams, unfailing loyalty to warlords, limited contact between men and women, and it turned those women into a commodity. It was this code that entrenched the system of revenge that flowed like a river down through the generations and was as unforgiving as the mountains and deserts of Afghanistan itself.

It was dark and silent. Hunt followed the tributary and water flowed downhill until the ground seemed to level out. He came into view of the lonesome compound and walked through one of the small holding's fields and felt the dry mud crunch under his boots. He stopped to listen. He felt like he was being watched. He was. Lambert would have been on the ledge for hours already. Watching the thermal image of his movements through the scope and tracing his every move.

The trees, high in the forest behind him, creaked and cracked as the breeze moved through them. Hunt came to the two meter high mud wall of the compound and listened. He heard nothing. It was always a risk, a covert entry into unknown property. Hunt was sure the farmer and his family were asleep. He was going to try and get what he needed and get out without disturbing them. Without waking them. Without drawing any attention to himself whatsoever. Like a ninja.

CHAPTER FIFTEEN

Hunt found the metal gate in the compound wall was bolted, but not locked. He gingerly and gently used his gloved hand to move the bolt. He eased backwards and put his left hand under the gate to lift some of the weight off the latch. The gate raised slightly against the tension of his forearm and shoulder. Hunt pulled it up and the bolt eased out mercifully quietly. Hunt held the gate and let the weight settle and then pushed it open. He slipped inside. Even Lambert wouldn't be able to see him now behind the wall.

Hunt had been prepared for loud and ferocious barking and was ready to have to silence a guard dog. But, there was no sound. Had he stumbled upon the only remote compound in Afghanistan without a vicious attack dog? He could only hope.

Hunt moved through the courtyard with his night vision goggles on. The highly-toxic green glow created an eerie image in his brain. He couldn't see any washing line, so he'd need to get inside.

Afghans tended not to have front doors. Instead, they hung heavy rugs in front of the openings in the walls of their houses. This made for easy and silent entry. But, the lack of certainty, the complete lack of knowledge, the complete unknown of what was behind the thick curtain started playing on his mind.

Hunt took the sling of the rifle off his shoulder and held it so that it was in the centre of his chest. He didn't want to kill anyone, but he also didn't know who was *really* in the house. For all he knew he could be walking into a room full of Taliban fighters. Hunt pulled the heavy rug-like curtain aside and ducked into the dark room.

AFTER HE ENTERED, HE CROUCHED AND HELD HIS BREATH. He heard the rapid thump of his heart and the swish of his blood in his ears. The whine of the night vision goggles sounded like a Rolls-Royce jet engine. The central room he was in opened up and had doors leading off into several other rooms running off in all directions. It looked like the kitchen was off to his left. The house had a smoky haze to it. A wood burner in another part of the house. Hunt felt his nose itch and held his breath again. He didn't want to sneeze. He scanned the room and noted the doors and entrances. It was cavernous and his movements made a dull echo on the mud walls.

He was looking for a laundry room, or a utility room, where the woman of the house kept her husband's dirty clothing. A key part of Hunt's deception would be to get a traditional Pashtun male dress and wear it in order to make the enemy think he was one of them. He heard a movement and swivelled to his right.

Through the night vision, Hunt saw a massive dog's head lift off its bedding and its ears pricked forward. Hunt froze. The two bright eyes shone like headlights in the green gloom of the goggles. Before he could say 'good boy' the giant *Jangi Spai* was up and on him. Hunt didn't have time to flick the safety off before the dog rushed at him. He had no leverage in his crouched position. The animal knocked him down on his back and onto the floor.

The Minimi spun away and went clattering across the clay-tiled floor. The dog went straight for his throat. Hunt brought his arm up to protect his face and neck and dipped his head so his Kevlar helmet would take the brunt of the bites as the dog gouged at him. He was aware of lights coming on in the house and then a woman screamed.

Hunt only had two options, one was to try and get away, but that was certain death. If he tried to move away from the oncoming force to try and create distance, the ferocity of the animal would overpower him and those fanged-jaws would be free to strike at the softest part of his body. Hunt would then be buried under the cabbages and his carcass left to rot. Maybe, this *Kucchi* would dig him up from time to time and have fun with his femur or jawbone. Hunt knew, like a fighter in a cage, his only other option was to get closer to his opponent.

Hunt wrapped his legs around the animal's lower back and locked his feet together. The Brazilian jiu-jitsu guys would have called it a 'closed guard'. He kept his helmet dipped. At first, the animal tried to rear away, but then it just got angrier and lunged down on him with its sharp claws and huge saliva-dripping canines, and tried to take chunks out of his face.

Hunt put his arm around the back of the dog's thick neck. He kept his chin tucked so his helmet faced the fangs. He took a scruff of the skin and fur and pulled himself right up close to the beast so its hot breath and black and yellow canines were pressed against his helmet. The animal thrashed wildly. There was shouting behind him and kids crying.

Hunt reached down with his right hand and felt for his

hip. He felt the nylon and the velcro of the holster and grabbed the grip of his Glock. He pulled the pistol up and stuck it in the dog's shoulder. He pulled the trigger repeatedly and the sound of the rounds smacking into muscle and bone made his ears ring. The massive hound squealed and backed off and instantly Hunt was up and spun in a crouch and raised his weapon. He lifted the night vision goggles. He had the handgun raised and steady. He was too slow.

The long grey-bearded farmer had picked up his discarded Minimi and was aiming it from his waist at Hunt. The farmer strained under the weight, but he was sinewy and fit from his years of back breaking work and Hunt heard the click of the safety as the farmer switched it off. Hunt had a fully automatic machine gun pointed at his torso. And this man knew what he was doing.

THERE WAS A STILLNESS. A CALM. LIKE THE HUSH THAT FELL over a congregation of the faithful, or when you lifted your face and listened to a wind blowing through the top of the trees.

The dog had crawled back to his bedding, which was just a rotten pile of discarded blankets and sheets. It licked its wounds and whimpered. Behind the farmer a mother held onto her children. It was silent, except for the giant brindle grey and dark black-striped hound.

The little girl wriggled in her mother's arms. Her father glanced at her.

"Aisha, no!" the mother screamed in Pashto as the little girl broke free from her arms and ran in front her father and towards her dog.

"Cujo!" she said and sprinted across the room and

wrapped herself around his neck. The dog licked her once on the head and she laughed.

The old farmer's face softened a little. The mother moved to retrieve her little girl and Hunt flicked the Glock's barrel at her and it told her to stay where she was. The woman sobbed and begged her daughter to return to her. The little girl sat next to her wounded pet and looked down and fingered the dog's blood on her pyjama top. Hunt wanted to move in an arc behind the girl and the dog, but he also didn't want to risk upsetting the beast of an animal again.

"Get out of my house," the farmer said quietly.

"Give me my gun," Hunt replied. He was stone faced and focussed. He was convinced he wasn't walking out of here. The old man raised his eyebrows. He was very surprised.

"You speak Pashto ..." he said and then went off on a flurry of rapid sentences that Hunt couldn't follow.

Hunt raised his voice, "Put the gun down, slowly," he said. He was sure the accent was terrible, but the old man seemed to get the message.

"What are you doing here!? Get out of my house, leave us alone," the woman screamed at Hunt between tears.

"I'll deal with this!" the old man said and glanced at his wife. He turned back to Hunt. "Do what she says, get out of her house!"

Hunt almost smiled and he saw a glint in the old man's eye. The matriarch was too worked up to share the unintentional joke. The situation was too tense.

"I don't want to hurt you," Hunt said. "I only wanted to borrow some ..." he searched for the word.

"Food," the man said.

"Not food," the wife countered. Her tone called him a moron. "Look at him, you think he would break into our house to steal bread? What do we have for him, nothing!" She shook her head after scolding her husband. Afghan women might have no rights, but in private they ruled the country, Hunt thought.

"... clothes," Hunt said.

"Give him your clothes," the woman demanded. Her husband turned to her and begged with his face, "Please, go in the bedroom. I am only wearing my sleep clothing. Don't tell me to take it off."

The little girl, all bloodied and tired, wobbled over to Hunt and showed him her outstretched index finger with the blood from her pyjama top on it. The old man lowered the weapon and put the safety on. Hunt took his finger off the trigger, but kept the handgun raised. The mother was in hysterics again.

"It's okay," Hunt said. "I'm not going to hurt her." He lifted the handgun to show its side to them and then holstered it. "I can repair your dog," he said. It was comical to the old man. "I have fixing tape." He pulled out an emergency medical kit from his webbing and held up the bandages. The man looked to his wife. She was silent and studied Hunt. There was no way out of this deadlock. Hunt could see that she knew it. She dipped her head and extended her arm out and said, "*Melmastyâ.*"

It meant simply *hospitality*, but also much more. *Melmastyâ* in the way she meant it was a virtue so as to be a point of national honour. It was an obligation under *pashtunwali*. Offered free and to be the same regardless whether the visitor was a stranger or member of their own tribe. The man's wife had just made Hunt an honorary guest in their home and the family was now duty bound to ensure his safety, even if it meant giving their own lives in order to ensure it.

"Put your guns away," she said. "I will put on the tea." And she walked to the kitchen.

CHAPTER SIXTEEN

Hunt mended the hound. The farmer muzzled it and held a cloth over its face and eyes and Hunt dug the rounds out of its thick shoulder muscle and then treated the wounds.

He gave it a jab of his morphine and it got dizzy and slept. Hunt was covered in the dog's blood and the farmer's wife offered him clean clothes. He gratefully accepted and wore the traditional Pashtun dress. He had his outfit. It smelled different. It smelled like the locals, and that was a good thing. The enemy couldn't tell the difference.

The women and children went to bed, Hunt and the farmer stayed awake to talk. They sat crossed-legged on Persian-style rugs and had a *Shura*. A consultation. They sat on the rugs in the living room and sipped tea from an ornate decorative tea set. The farmer said his name was Pamir. He welcomed Hunt into his home and thanked him for fixing his dog.

"He's a good dog," Hunt said. "He'll make a full recovery."

He knew the dog was only doing his job and he felt terrible; but it was a tough old beast and it would heal completely.

As Hunt's adrenaline filtered out of his system, he started to feel more uncomfortable about the situation.

After all, he'd intruded into the man's house, shot his dog, and scared his children. And, despite that, Hunt now sat cross-legged on a Persian-rug with the very man whose house he had broken into, sharing stories, and drinking tea. He'd never known anything like it. The commitment to this level of community and hospitality was alien to him except amongst the family of farm labourers on their ranch in the Eastern Highlands of what used to be Rhodesia and was now Zimbabwe.

They discussed many things. First, and rightly, the farmer asked about why Hunt and the soldiers were in his country. Considering Hunt was probably the first white face that Pamir had spoken to directly, it was a fair question.

Hunt was more than likely the first westerner he had ever had in his house. Pamir said, "I don't support the Taliban, but I also cannot support foreign invaders in our country, no matter the reason for them being here."

He told Hunt that his grandfather had fought against the Prince of Wales Royal Regiment in the mid-nineteenth century. And he wondered whether Hunt and the fellow British Army soldiers were there to take revenge for the blood spilled by the Afghans against the British in the wars of the eighteen-fifties. Blood feuds never end. Revenge as a reason for war was something that these people understood all too well. Hunt tried to reassure him that the western armies were only in Pashtunistan to catch Osama bin Laden.

"But," Pamir said, "bin Laden is not in this village ... so why are you here?"

It was a good question. Hunt didn't have an answer. He did have a story which would fit with the culture of blood feuds that Pamir could understand though. Hunt told him the story of his fiancée. That she'd been taken from him; killed violently, by a man that was in the village. Pamir listened intently to the story. And, after Hunt finished telling him about his quest to get revenge for her, Pamir considered the importance of the tale. In the story, to help him better understand, he called Kelly his wife. But, even though she was his fiancée, in Hunt's mind, it was accurate. He would always be in love with her.

The old farmer and Hunt looked into one another's eyes and there was an understanding from the old Pashtun man and the young British soldier. Pamir said he would help. Not to help destroy the Taliban, but because Hunt was his guest and someone to be protected, Pamir said he would help him achieve his goal. Hunt assured the old farmer that he did not know the man that Hunt intended to kill. Hunt told him that the man was a foreigner. A Muslim. Not Taliban. Not from Afghanistan.

Pamir was satisfied that it was within custom and that even though this man whom Hunt wished to kill was not an enemy, he was not a welcome guest in Afghanistan. The old farmer then made a suggestion. At dawn, which was only a few short hours away, the farmer was going into the village with his wooden wheelbarrow to set up a market stall in the main street.

Hunt knew the street he was talking about, he'd observed it through his scope earlier on the previous day. The mosque was at the far end of it and the pale-blue compound gate was near the middle of it. It was a long straight dusty road that Hunt had looked down on for most of the day. He knew it well. The farmer suggested that Hunt accompany him, in disguise, like he was now, to see if he would be able to find the man he sought. Identify him and then leave.

Hunt thought about it and nearly leaned over the table and kissed Pamir on the cheek. He thought it was an excellent idea. He did have a question in his mind about what he would do with his combat gear and rifle though.

Hunt enquired as to whether the old farmer had a weapon. Pamir stood from his cross-legged position like a much younger man. He was still strong. He disappeared into one of the other rooms, in the quiet and now dark house. His wife and children slept in the adjoining rooms. Pamir returned with a polished AK-47.

"I have had it since the war with the Russians," Pamir said proudly. He handed the weapon to Hunt. Hunt took it and checked it over. It was a classic piece of equipment, in classic shape. If it was a vintage car it would be in showroom condition.

Hunt went to hand the rifle back to Pamir, but he refused. He shook his hands back and forth and refused to accept the weapon. He didn't say it, but he intended for Hunt to keep it. That's what Hunt understood from the transaction, anyway.

Hunt said thank you Pashto. In turn, Hunt went to his kit which was placed in a neat pile next to him in the living room. He unloaded the Minimi and made it safe, before holding it out, and handing it to Pamir. Hunt was swapping weapons with the farmer.

"Can we switch back, or exchange once again, when we have finished our business?" Hunt asked, the old man agreed.

It was nearly light. Hunt and the old farmer had already spoken for many hours. There was a dark blue hue coming in through the windows and Hunt could feel the crisp morning air. Dawn was nearly on the horizon and the coldness of the valley would soon warm. Hunt and the farmer went out to prepare his cart for the market.

The farmer suggested that Hunt go ahead of him to the village and find a place near the mosque where he could wait for life in the village to start. The old farmer told him that the Taliban fighters slept in the local mosque when they came to invade villages. They wanted to rule people with legitimate control, so they did not harass people in their homes.

In return, however, the villagers were expected to provide food and clothing for the soldiers. Hunt had seen many of the al-Qaeda and Taliban soldiers the day before. They had black turbans around their heads and faces and wore heavy camouflaged military jackets and overcoats over their thick traditional robes. They wore different designs of camouflage from different countries. Many of them had combat gloves and almost all of them carried either AK-74s or AK-47s. Hunt saw some rocket propelled grenade launchers slung over shoulders and many of the Taliban fighters drove around the village in gangs on scooters and mopeds.

As it was market day in the village, the old farmer said that Hunt could expect it to be very busy. He would have a better chance of blending in and concealing himself in the mass of people as the fighters bought food, ammunition, clothes, and other things from the locals. Hunt said he would stay in the village, out of sight, he planned to sit near, but not with the farmer on the market street and keep an eye out for al-Zawahiri.

The two men shook hands.

CHAPTER SEVENTEEN

HUNT HAD WALKED AHEAD from the farmer's compound to the village. It was a fair distance. It was still dark when he arrived and he felt nervous, like he'd arrived too early for a day at school and the place was still eerie and overly quiet.

He anticipated the danger he would be in if he was found. He'd borrowed the farmer's turban and wrapped it around his head and face in the traditional manner. He'd seen the soldiers at the checkpoints dressed in the same way and it would not be out of place. The only thing showing were his grey eyes.

He had the farmer's traditional robes and the farmer's wife had wrapped a blanket, or cape, around his shoulders to keep him warm in the dull winter sun. His AK-47 was slung over one shoulder, nonchalantly, in the Pashtun manner. Hunt had his pistol in its holster strapped next to his skin on his waist. It was concealed under the robe and the cold tip of the gun touched the top of his pubic bone. It was a bit uncomfortable but, as long as he didn't accidentally blow his balls off, he could deal with it. If the farmer's rifle failed to fire for any reason Hunt had a back-up. A hard-to-reach back-up.

He was playing this piece of the concerto purely by ear. If the opportunity arose, he would decide in the moment whether to take it or not. He might be able to halt the al-Qaeda threat in its tracks right then and there. And it would all have been worth it. Everyone wanted bin Laden, but Hunt had seen reports and knew from the methodology of the guy that Osama might be the face of al-Qaeda, but Doctor Ayman al-Zawahiri was the brains. He planned the Twin Towers attack.

Dawn broke and the *Fajir*, the sunrise prayer, blared out over the village and rang out in a dull drone into the valley. It was the first of five prayer sessions throughout the day. It was a rude awakening. Some time after the dawn prayer, people drifted lazily into the streets. Once the sun was up, it didn't take long for the village to bustle.

THE *BAZAAR* WAS A BIG ATTRACTION. AS THE PEOPLE walked up and down the road they created a fine film of dust which floated in the sunlight and came to rest over the produce.

People didn't seem to care. The sellers lined the street where taxis arrived and brought people from other nearby villages. The street was lined with stainless steel stands with umbrellas and men pushed them up and down the street selling food. Hunt saw a butcher with full-sized carcasses of goats and sheep hanging from a wooden shipping-sized container. Other men sold fruit and vegetables from stands and used horse tail-hair fly whips to chase away the flies that hovered and landed around the food. Hunt sat in the shade next to a wall and observed the people. He looked down and tried not to make eye contact with anyone. No-one paid him much attention.

One thing that immediately struck Hunt was the number of young children around. More than half of the village seem to be under the age of fifteen. Kids played in the streets with tyres. Groups of young boys played with marbles. And later there was a game of cricket going on in one of the open bits of land behind the shopping street. The Afghans seemed to love cricket and Hunt wondered whether the British had brought them the game when they first tried to invade this country in the 1840s.

Something changed mid-morning. The games stopped. Quiet came over the village. There were rumours being passed around. Hunt overheard snippets of conversation that there was a foreign soldier nearby. Then there was another conversation that a foreign soldier had been captured. He heard some women talking under their *burqas* about an enemy soldier that had been captured and they were afraid. Hunt wondered whether they were somehow talking about him and the gossip was confused and he became paranoid.

If anyone looked in his direction his immediate thought was to jump up and run. He had to keep his cool because as soon as he reacted, any attention he brought on himself, he would be murdered. Then, there was a noise from the north side of the village. There was chanting and ululating and men fired AK-47s into the air. A big throng of people came down the main street carrying a body on their shoulders. The old farmer came over to Hunt and pulled him up by the shoulder and told him to look.

"Go and look, go and look, this is one of yours..." That was all the old farmer said and he proceeded to pack his stall away as men and boys ran towards the mob. Hunt gingerly and nervously observed the crowd of people as they passed him. He stepped back into a small alleyway between the buildings and watched the throng move past.

Oh, God. Hunt saw a soldier's boots and he recognised

the uniform. It was a Foreign Legion uniform. Then he saw the hair, the head flopped to the side. No! Hunt thought. His heart sank, he wanted to scream and run to the crowd and pull the body off the men's shoulders and tell them to stop shaking him. It was Lambert.

Hunt followed the procession. They paraded the body in the streets. He couldn't tell if Lambert was dead or alive, but he was bleeding from his nose and ears and his hair was matted.

They threw the body in the street and a crowd of people began stomping it. They were chanting 'Death to infidels! Death to infidels!' as they took turns kicking and punching the lifeless body. Hunt didn't know what to do. He had to save him. al-Qaeda soldiers were trying to clear the crowd. A man hit Hunt in the side of the turban with the stock of his rifle and screamed at him to get away.

Suddenly, there was a deafening blast of gunfire from an automatic rifle. The crowd went silent and parted. Hunt got up and scampered away to blend into the crowd again. One of the al-Qaeda street commanders in his traditional robes and military camouflage jacket held up his AK-47. He spoke loudly and with authority he claimed the body of the prisoner for Mullah Dadullah. No one was to further injure the prisoner until the council had decided what they were going to do with him. Hunt took this as a good sign, because it meant that Lambert was more than likely still alive, even if he probably wished he was dead.

CHAPTER EIGHTEEN

Hunt had lots of questions. If Lambert was alive, he was in grave danger. Had Lambert managed to get comms with the ops room? Had he given them a SITREP? Did they know where they were?

Hunt glanced up at the surrounding mountains, he could see that none of the other sniper teams had line of sight to his current position. Hunt had to keep a close eye on Lambert. Forget trying to assassinate al-Zawahiri now. If Lambert was alive, Hunt had to find a way to save him.

The Taliban fighters brought a rudimentary stretcher and placed the unconscious body onto it. Other Taliban fighters, also wearing combat jackets, used their weapons to push the crowd back and create a path through them. The stretcher bearers lifted Lambert's body in one go and moved off at a shuffle, forward, through the crowd. They took Lambert towards the mosque. It was doubling as the Taliban headquarters. The mosque was the largest and most ornate building in the village. It had a tall tower with three blue speakers at the top. That was where they blasted the five daily prayers out to the faithful.

The men carrying the body shuffled and strained against the weight and made their way through the gates to the mosque. They took the body inside. Hunt followed along with the crowd of people. They were drawn to the prisoner and the soldiers moving him towards the tall building.

The crowd filled it up from the front until the only space left was outside the gates. Some stood around the windows of the building. Local children put their hands up to the glass and peered through the decorative windows into the wooden and intricately painted interior.

Hunt found a way to push past some people and slip inside. He stood at the back of the room and checked for exits. He needed a way out. They'd put Lambert on a medical table at the far end of the mosque that had been set up as a medical bay. They had a screen across the body and it looked like some local Taliban or al-Qaeda medics had supplies there.

There was a doctor with a stethoscope and turban who assessed Lambert. While that was going on the mosque filled with more people, they were polite and gentle, but they were ushered back and kept at bay by the Taliban security. One of the Taliban commanders came and stood at the front and ordered everybody to sit down and be quiet while they gathered.

Then, Hunt saw his enemy again, at a much closer range this time. Al-Zawahiri and Mullah Dadullah were part of a group of about ten older Taliban commanders and village elders. Hunt felt his blood rise. He held his breath. All of a sudden he felt warm under the robes. He tried to keep a clear mind, but seeing al-Zawahiri made his stress and anger levels rise. He loved it. The elders sat around in a circle on a rug and conducted the tribal formalities of the conversation around the capture of the prisoner. They would discuss it as a group and come to a conclusion. It was a *shura*, a consultation, and tea was a vital element.

From what Hunt could hear of the conversation and some of the whispering in the audience, he understood that one of the Taliban patrols in the surrounding mountains had captured Lambert as he tried to traverse back through the mountain pass.

The Taliban perimeter security had heard the helicopters from the time that Hunt and Lambert had infiltrated the mountains, and they'd been scouring the mountainous countryside surrounding the village ever since. Hunt realised that he and Lambert were likely to have been discovered at some point over the next several days *anyway*. Maybe they would have been ambushed. Maybe they would be dead instead.

It was a roll of the dice that they hadn't had any radio communications with the ops room. If Hunt had been with Lambert, he was under no illusions that he too would be lying on an operating table. Maybe a mortuary table.

The conversation moved on, and the village elders, Taliban, and al-Qaeda representatives discussed what to do with the prisoner. Al-Zawahiri wanted al-Qaeda to claim ownership of the body and use it to send a message. He wanted to decapitate Lambert in front of a camera and send it to the world's media to show the power and force and ruthlessness of al-Qaeda to the people who dared to interfere.

The elders were silent, but Mullah Dadullah made it clear that he was not convinced. He was the senior Taliban commander. Al-Qaeda were his guests. He believed that the prisoner belonged to the rulers of the country. Mullah Dadullah believed that it was more beneficial to use the prisoner to gain information about enemy movements and enemy plans. He wanted to interrogate the prisoner and find out where the enemy were and what they were planning. Mullah

Dadullah wanted to know how many soldiers were surrounding them and whether they could expect an attack. He made it clear that their strategic priority was to attack and recapture Mazar-i-Sharif and that the prisoner would be more useful as a hostage, or as a tool to negotiate with the western invaders.

All of the men nodded in solemn agreement. Dadullah then spoke loudly to the audience and he told them that the *shura* agreed that the foreign invaders were sentimental and soft and not true warriors. He told them that their enemy would be open to a discussion in order to save the life of one of their soldiers. The conversation continued.

CHAPTER NINETEEN

HUNT STAYED QUIET AND STILL. He was hidden in plain sight. He rubbed the side of his head with his palm and tried to think. His heart thumped loudly in his chest. He was sweating. He felt like they could smell the fear on him. He kept checking his periphery. One of the al-Qaeda guards kept looking at him. Did he somehow know? Did he suspect.

There was movement behind the white cotton medical screen. Hunt watched. Out of the corner of his eye he saw the terrorist guard looking at him and stroking his long beard. He watched Hunt. Hunt's cover was blown. He just knew it. He *felt* it. The artery thumping in his neck told him so. The sweat running down from his brow and onto his lip told him so.

For some reason all he could hear was heavy metal rock music in his head. The distorted screaming of rage. Was he about to do something reckless? He took some long, slow, deep breaths. They were moving Lambert's body. The *shura* was still going on and the men continued discussing things. A lot of sombre nodding and open palmed hand gestures. People started to leave. Hunt'd heard enough. He understood that closed-eyed, sombre-nodding meant agreement. It had been decided.

Now Hunt needed to see where they were moving the body to. He moved sideways, stepping through the people still sitting on the floor. The mosque was a cramped space and filled with onlookers interested in the outcome. Hunt wasn't sure if they were mostly villagers, or Taliban, or a mix. He had to walk past the al-Qaeda guard to get out of the building. Hunt glanced up as he moved through the cross-legged crowd. Hunt saw that the guard had his dark, dark, eyes trained on him.

The guard made a move like he was about to approach Hunt. Hunt looked down and away as he moved through the rows of people on the floor. He would have to pass the guard at any moment. He walked past him. He walked out of the mosque and was heading down the stairs and fighting the temptation to run when he felt someone grab his right arm. He was caught. He panicked. He wanted to run. He wanted to fight. Hunt stopped and slowly turned his head. The guard said, "How's your head brother?"

Hunt's heart beat against his rib cage, fast and hard. Suddenly, in his fog of panic, Hunt realised; the guard was the same guy who'd battered him in the side of the head with the stock of his rifle. He'd tried to crack Hunt's head open as he protected Lambert from the angry mob. Hunt raised his hand to his head and mumbled, "It's okay, it's okay..." in Pashto and tried to keep a normal walking pace as he moved away from the mosque.

A crowd of people had gathered in front of the mosque and in the streets. It seemed like the whole village had been drawn to the mosque to hear the outcome of the discussion between the elders. Hunt saw the stretcher and a group of people, including the doctor, leaving the mosque through a back entrance. Then he lost them. Hunt started walking stealthily to try and follow the group and follow Lambert. The streets were empty with everyone drawn to the *shura*.

THE PROCESSION WAS GONE. HUNT ONLY SAW ONE OTHER guard in a multi-terrain pattern winter jacket with a long beard and turban on. The man was on his haunches, tearing apart some flatbread and chewing it listlessly. Sentry was a boring job wherever it is. Afghans had no qualms about sleeping on duty. Hunt tried to make it look like he was on official business and in a hurry, but when the al-Qaeda guard saw him, he stood up and said something, through a mouthful of bread, which Hunt didn't understand.

"Dammit," Hunt said under his breath and started walking towards the guard. He didn't know if he'd been summoned over, but if he had, he didn't want to disobey this man and cause a scene. Hunt pulled out a packet of pink chewing gum as he walked up to the guard. He always carried gum, a pack of smokes, and a knife. They could get you out of most situations. He loosened one of the silver paper wrapped pieces of pink gum and walked up to the flatbread-eating guard.

His number one way of getting found out was to open his mouth and speak. He had no choice. He walked right up to the guard and said in his best impression of a Taliban brother, "Did you see where they took the infidel?"

The man swallowed his flatbread and took the stick of gum that Hunt held out to him. The man stuffed it lengthwise into his mouth and lifted his chin down the road. He chewed and eyed Hunt with suspicion. It was the compound that Hunt had seen al-Zawahiri and Dadullah come out of the previous day. He recognised the high walls and the solid, reinforced, pale-blue metal gate. Hunt knew it must belong to somebody with influence in the village, because it was in prime position and so central to the rest of the village. A compound within a compound.

The guard turned back to him from looking down the street and said, "Where are you from?"

Pashtuns were native to the southern eastern regions of Afghanistan. Hunt didn't know what to say. He didn't want to be drawn into a round of small talk with a guard, so he said, "Where is your station?"

He looked surprised to be challenged, but he said, "I'm guarding the main street. Where do you come from?" the guard asked again.

"Why do you ask?" Hunt said.

"You sound different by your accent ..." he said and put one hand on the back of the rifle slung across his chest. Hunt smiled and hoped the smile lines around his eyes would show the guard he was friendly and no threat.

"Show me your face," the guard said. "Who are you? What's your name?"

Hunt hesitated and said, "Excuse me?" and hoped it wasn't a strange thing to say. He wanted to imply that he hadn't heard what the man had said. The man grabbed his rifle and went to yell for help. Hunt hit the guard at the top of his windpipe and then grabbed the weapon. Hunt didn't want the guard to get any purchase. Hunt used the rifle to push the man backward and overpowered him. The guard gagged from the blow to his throat.

Hunt manoeuvred himself behind the guard and put his forearm on his Adam's apple and squeezed. Hunt's forearm was like a guillotine. It chopped off the air supply and the man struggled and kicked out and tried to pull Hunt's arm away. It was no use. The fear of death and intense adrenaline kick meant Hunt was an immovable force. There was no way he would let go, or give up. It wasn't an option. As the man's panic peaked his face scrunched up in twisted agony and then his body went limp. His head stayed upright because of the force on his neck. Hunt was gasping for air. It was a fight to the death. He didn't lose those.

Hunt breathed deeply and felt the burn of the cold thin air in his lungs. It was exhausting operating at this elevated altitude. Through the sweat in his eyes, Hunt looked around to see if anybody had witnessed the murder. He got up quickly and pulled the body down a nearby alleyway. He covered the body in a tarpaulin and pulled over some broken pieces of wood and half a tyre that was strewn around. He was in a hurry, but content that it was concealed.

"What a waste of gum," he said and walked out of the alleyway and dusted himself off and looked at the compound where they held Lambert.

CHAPTER TWENTY

Hunt felt like he was quickly losing control of this situation. If he had had any control to begin with. He'd have to bend it to his will. He'd have to dig deep and use his resources. He needed comms. He needed backup. He needed help but no one was coming. He was alone in this viper's nest.

Hunt took up the position where the guard had been. He kept an eye on the compound for a few minutes, and then, he heard activity.

There was chattering from the rabble of people as they left *shura* and spilled out of the mosque and into the dusty street. Hunt decided to move positions. He went along the main street where the market had been. He found a small alleyway that was no more than a gap in between two compound walls. It was littered with crushed plastic bottles, broken cinder blocks, old bicycle tyres, and wet and rotting leaves. It smelled like men, dogs, and goats had used it as a public toilet.

Hunt backed into the narrow alleyway and crouched. He saw people streaming back into the streets and there was an excited chatter from the village. He saw groups of al-Qaeda storm troopers marching around. They stopped people in the street, mostly older men and women with full face coverings on. The women became upset and irate and told them to back off and get away, but the bearded black-turbaned terrorist guards forced them to remove their headdresses and uncover their faces.

Afterwards the women were allowed to put the *burkas* and face coverings back on and they left and hurried away. The village was abuzz; the thin air grew dusty again and the particles floated around on still air. Hunt felt he was in mortal danger. He had to leave, he knew he had to leave, but, like watching a fatal car crash, he also couldn't take his eyes away from the pale-blue painted door which led into the compound where Lambert had been taken.

Hunt nearly jumped out of his skin. Someone, behind the wall to his right, had said something to him in Pashto. Hunt leaned forward slightly and poked his head out from the alleyway. Leaning up against the building next to the alley was the same man who had battered him in the side in the head with the butt of his rifle. The same guy who had tried to apologise to him at the mosque was now speaking to him while Hunt hid in a filthy ablution alley.

"I don't understand?" Hunt said in Pashto. He swallowed hard and hoped his accent and pronunciation and cadence was passable. Hunt didn't notice any change in the al-Qaeda soldier's expression.

"I said, what are you doing here?" the man repeated. Hunt stood slowly from his squatting position and when he was upright, the soldier said, "Remove your face covering please."

Hunt didn't move. He wasn't breathing. His mind was blank. Just when he needed a plan. He remembered he had his pistol cradled on his groin. The robes and the heavy clothes would make the manoeuvre to pull the pistol more difficult. And he had to reach up and under the robes to get access. It was still a good insurance policy, but the process for cashing it in was complicated. And, because he'd backed himself into the alley, bringing the AK-47 to bear would be difficult, if he fired it, it would draw a lot of attention.

"We're checking everyone in the village. The Doctor thinks there could be infiltrators amongst us. We are checking *everyone* ... You saw. Even the women are being checked. So now, let me check."

Hunt had no choice. He very slowly raised his hand to his right ear where the turban was tightly tucked in. As soon as he removed it and showed his face, he knew he was done for. Maybe it was just an inevitability, maybe he was already done for, before he even removed the turban.

Either way, it didn't matter. It was over. It felt like defeat. This was the end of the road. He'd only managed to get within sight of al-Zawahiri. The fact that he'd even managed to get within sight of the al-Qaeda deputy was more than any westerner had ever achieved. It was also now irrelevant. Hunt was going to lose, again, to the man who had taken everything from him.

His only other option was to use his rifle as a club and disable the soldier with it. His enemy was alert and had his own weapon at his side. The al-Qaeda fighter was confident, like he was dealt a pair of aces at the poker table. The bearded soldier stopped leaning and stood upright as Hunt's hand moved further towards his right ear. In a slick movement, the Afghan slipped his shoulder out of the sling. He held the rifle across his chest. Hunt didn't bother taking off the turban in the end. He thought, if I'm going down, I'm taking another one of you bastards with me. Hunt charged out of the narrow gap in the alleyway and into the Al-Qaeda soldier.

Hunt grabbed onto the AK-47 rifle and used it to push

the soldier backwards. The man was shocked at first, then resisted and shouted for help. Hunt could smell his breath and his beard as he pushed his head and body into the terrorist. Hunt was surprised by the man's strength. The soldier pinned his back leg and straightened it. His foot slipped in the dust as he resisted Hunt's charge. Hunt got himself into the position he wanted. He pinned his leg behind the al-Qaeda soldier's leg, and drove his right shoulder into his chest. They both went down hard. As they fell the al-Qaeda soldier squeezed on the AK-47's trigger. Hunt felt the mechanism working against his chest muscles as rounds exploded into the compound wall beside them. The sound was deafening.

The wind left the guy's lungs as he hit the ground square with his shoulders and the back of his head cracked against it. Hunt put his hand on the soldier's trigger finger and twisted it backwards to stop the weapon from firing. While still holding onto the guy's finger, Hunt drove his right elbow into the side of the terrorist's face. He screamed out as his finger snapped back and nearly broke off. Hunt kept on pounding him in the side of the face and head with his elbow. He could hear the crack of his sharp elbow bone against the terrorist's cheek and nose. The guy's head bounced off the compacted dust with every strike. It was a complete blur of ferocity. An attack by a feral beast. Hunt kept hitting him over and over.

The next thing Hunt felt were hands on his back, shoulders, and turban pulling him off. They wrenched him off the soldier. The crowd gathered and was soon full of men wearing multi-terrain pattern camouflage jackets. They were al-Qaeda. Some others were in the regular dress of the villagers. It didn't matter, they started kicking and punching him.

The force of the blows dropped Hunt to his knees, and he was quickly overwhelmed by a crowd of people pushing forward, throwing punches and kicks. Sometimes you just have to tuck your chin and knees and accept the landing. He was accepting it now as people jumped, kicked, punched, and threw stones at him.

It felt like it went on for twelve rounds, but it was probably over in a matter of seconds. Hunt felt himself being lifted roughly out of the dry dust. His turban had been ripped off. His clothing was covered in dust and his beard was caked with dirt and blood. As he was being held in place, people spat at him and threw dirt in his face. The punches and kicks he'd taken to the stomach made him want to retch. Hunt fully expected to be pushed to his knees and executed in the unforgiving Afghan desert right then and right there.

He couldn't stand on his own. He felt like he might have ruptured his spleen, or had some spinal cord damage. His legs were weak. They took him away. His feet dragged behind him in the dust. It took five men struggling under his weight to drag him towards the pale-blue compound gate. The one Hunt had seen al-Zawahiri come out of. The one Lambert was in.

He was handled roughly. The pale-blue gate was only wide enough for two of them to pass through at once, the width of a single door. The pallbearers weren't sure how to get him through. So they stood arguing outside the gates and left him lying in the dirt. Eventually, two of them tried to take a run up and force their way through, one holding him on each side. They took a run up, but only Hunt and one other made it.

One of the men carrying him smacked his head into the open metal gate. Hunt went down face first into the courtyard floor.

CHAPTER TWENTY-ONE

Hunt found himself slumped on a small metal chair. His head lolled forward and his cheek rested against a shoulder, like a drunk sitting passed out leaning against a wall.

He wasn't sure whether he'd even managed to put his arm out to protect his face from the floor or not. Probably not, judging by the pain in his cheek. He sat there in pain trying to recover some energy and work out how bad his injuries were. His arms hung down by his side. He managed to open one of his puffed-up eyes and saw Lambert sitting in front of him.

Lambert had his hands tied behind his back. He had dried blood all over his face, and all over the front of his badly torn uniform. Besides the injuries, he somehow looked different to Hunt in this light. The light came from a rectangular window high above his left shoulder and a bright yellow bulb placed in the corner behind where Hunt sat. Somewhere a generator chugged away. Lambert looked like he was in a terrible state.

Hunt stayed like he was, trying to survey the room, and work out what kind of position they found themselves in. Dire. He wondered when they'd found Lambert. He must've been trying to get comms with the headquarters when he was discovered and attacked.

Hunt swallowed and tasted the blood in his mouth from his bleeding tongue and gums. Should he have made a different decision? That didn't matter now. The past didn't exist. Only surviving, by any means necessary, mattered now. He was in the worst place he could possibly have imagined. There were three heavyset Pashtun men in the room with them. They were having a discussion.

Hunt wondered whether he could grab the handgun before they noticed he was awake. But, then what? It didn't look like Lambert was in any condition to move. Hunt would have to free him before any other guards or al-Qaeda realised he was loose.

Too late. The fattest one from the group noticed Hunt's eyes move and mentioned it to the other two. He was awake. The fat one walked up to Hunt and whacked him across the face with the back of his chubby hand. There was a loud clap and Hunt's face stung. It felt like being hit with a plank.

One of the others went behind him and grabbed him roughly by his wrists. Hunt struggled and kept his arms rigid and tried to keep his hands as far apart as possible. The guard behind him handled him roughly and tied his wrists together. Hunt flexed his muscles to try and create as much tension as possible, and keep the bindings loose. The rough rope was pulled tight and Hunt immediately felt the blood swell in his fingers. When they were ready one of the guards opened the thin wooden door and called out, "He's ready for you..."

A man that Hunt hadn't seen before entered the room. He was tall with a hooked nose. He was more elegantly dressed than most people Hunt had seen. He stepped into the room and stood in front of Hunt. The guards looked at him reverently and backed away, like he had a force field around him.

"Have you searched him?" the newcomer asked.

One of the guards made a movement towards Hunt, while the fat one and the other glanced at one another. They hadn't done their job. They looked like they were hoping they wouldn't find anything on him as their colleague patted Hunt down. He didn't have a clue what he was doing. This guy must have thought Hunt was boobytrapped, because he was paranoid and very agitated. He felt around Hunt's neck and then pulled out a knife. He held it in front of Hunt's face and grinned at him with disgusting yellow and black teeth. Hunt moved his face to the side to avoid the smell. The guard pulled out his tags and cut them off and handed them to the tall, white-bearded one. Hunt suddenly felt more vulnerable without them, like he was standing naked in front of a crowd. Now he was sterile. A body with no name. No identification. Nothing to say who he was when they found his stripped, beaten, half-skinned, naked corpse in a ditch. They'd just taken away his identity. Then the guard lifted out the two syrettes of morphine that hung around his neck. The smile on this guard widened and he jumped around like a chicken trying to evade a fox. He was cock-a-hoop at the prospect that he and the boys would be shooting it up later. They loved opium here and it grew everywhere, one of the few things that will. Was it the hardiness of the flower that gave it its powers? The toughness that produced elation. Crushing pressure made diamonds. Hunt decided it was. And he would tough this out. Pressure only makes diamonds.

If they were doing this properly they would have taken Hunt's clothes off. Instead he sat there enduring a rub down with the strong smells of burnt coffee, cheap cigarettes, and floral scented soap. Part of him felt like it wasn't real. Like this was happening to someone else. It was his mind creating a reality distortion field. Hunt had never once thought about something like this happening to himself. He never thought it could. He felt a sense of disbelief. As if he had been driving down the road and knocked a little girl off her bicycle. It was a willingness to not want to believe it. Hunt gritted his teeth and clenched his muscles. He felt the handgun lodged against his lower stomach.

The guard turned to the tall gentleman and said, "No. Nothing."

The tall man moved directly in front of Hunt and, silently, slowly sank to his haunches. While in a low squat, he took hold of the bottom of Hunt's robes, and flipped them up and over his knees, like he was flicking a blanket. So what's it going to be, terrifying torture or am I about to get screwed? Men in Afghanistan were notorious for buggering young boys at special parties. Hunt couldn't see why they wouldn't rape a prisoner.

The man reached in with two hands like he was about to deliver a baby, but instead pulled out Hunt's concealed handgun. He held it up for the guards to see. The fat guard swatted his colleague on the back of his head.

"You can never be too careful with these infidels," the tall man said knowingly and stood and the guards nodded in agreement. Mostly, the guards just seemed relieved that they weren't going to get flogged for the mistake. The tall man stuck the nylon holstered pistol into the waistband of his outfit and said to the guards, "I only need one of you to stay. You'll be stationed outside the door. Are any of you not moving out with the rest of the brothers?"

The tall man turned and looked back at Hunt and said in Pashto, "Do you understand me?"

Hunt didn't react, but he could just about follow the conversation. The tall man turned back to the guards and said, "Go now, we will decide what to do with these enemies."

Hunt understood by what the tall man had said, that the

majority of the fighters were leaving the village. They must know that they'd been seen. And so, they were leaving, but where to?

The danger was that they were bringing the attack forward and starting the recapture of Mazar-i-Sharif. Hunt had no idea whether any of the other sniper teams would see the troop movement or not. Was anyone aware besides him?

He *had* to warn the headquarters, and his friends and colleagues in Mazar, as soon as possible. The Taliban and al-Qaeda army could be in sight of the town within hours. They could be there by nightfall. Hunt had less than five hours to warn them of the danger.

THE FAT GUARD NODDED TO HIS LEADER AND SAID, "I WILL remain here," and ushered the other two guards out of the room. He closed the door behind him. The tall man slowly turned towards Hunt and said in Pashto, "You managed to infiltrate our village ..."

Hunt tried to speak, but his swollen tongue and cut lips made forming vowels difficult. He decided against talking. There was no way Lambert would have gone into his cover story yet. The 'big four' answers allowed under the Geneva Convention on Prisoners of War. Name, rank, serial number, date of birth. Hunt doubted they would be familiar with it, or abide by it. The tall man switched to speaking English. He said again, "How did you manage to infiltrate our village?"

He spoke excellent English, even his accent was westernised. It was possible that he had studied abroad, it had more of an English lilt than an American one, but it retained the cultural undertones of the Middle Eastern accent, although it was barely detectable. His diction was very precise.

"How did you come to find us?"

Hunt didn't answer. The man paced with his hands clasped behind his back. Hunt watched him from under his puffed up eyelids and was silent. He knew that they were just getting warmed up. That's what the fat man outside the interrogation room door was for.

"How many of you are there?"

Each time he asked a question he would look at Hunt, stop mid-pace, before looking away, lifting his chin and stepping forward to continue pacing. It was as if he was in an office, dictating a letter to his secretary.

"How did you come by this information?" the man said, "By that, I mean, where did the intelligence come from that you found our village?" He glanced at Hunt again and paced.

"What is your name?"

"Stirling."

Hunt knew that he could answer that question.

The tall man nodded approvingly.

"What's your religion?"

Hunt thought about it. He could have said, 'I cannot answer that question'. Instead, he decided to say, "Christian."

It was inscribed on his dog tags as Church of England, so he didn't see the harm. They had the information already, even if they didn't know it. To the Taliban, if you weren't a Sunni, you weren't a Muslim. In fact, Hunt was safer saying he was a Christian, because under Sharia Law, he had to pay a tax for being an infidel. Whereas the Shia minority were seen as fair game to execute on the spot. Ancient Greek logic had failed to reach this far into the mountains of Afghanistan.

"How is my English, by the way," the tall man said.

"Very good," Hunt said.

"Yes, I thought you might think as much. I am Abdullah bin Mohammed." He said it as if Hunt was supposed to recognise the name, but he didn't. Hunt picked him for a Jordanian, or a Sunni from Persia. The Taliban and al-Qaeda drew followers and recruits from far and wide. Religious fanatics who became fighters, who in turn became politicians. "I was at your Royal Military Academy Sandhurst," he said. "Her Majesty's armed forces trained me."

Hunt boiled inside. This man was smirking at him. Rubbing his face in it.

"Yeah, well, every hat I met from the army officer corps was a pongo."

"I'm sorry, I don't get your meaning."

Hunt shook his head. Better not to piss this guy off and risk another filling in. He wasn't sure of the Taliban's record of extreme mistreatment of prisoners, but he'd heard enough stories about what al-Qaeda did to captured soldiers.

There were stories of them crucifying soldiers. Stringing them up by their limbs and torturing them with a kind of mediaeval brutality long since forgotten in other parts of the world. The victim's skin would be flayed and pulled back while they were alive; and the Islamic student brothers would use them as human urinals. The smell must've been horrendous. The flies and maggots that resulted from the stench was enough to make him think that it was worth putting a pistol in his mouth and pulling the trigger rather than endure that.

That was what they'd been recommended to do, 'unofficially'. Some of the CIA intelligence guys had said to him, "If you ever happen to get captured by those bastards, *remember* it's better to pull the trigger and blow your brains out than let them capture you." Yeah, cheers. Thanks for the advice fellas.

Hunt just hoped that this man was more political than he was religious.

"You beat one of our brothers very badly," Abdullah said. "What do you have to say about that?"

Hunt just glared at him.

"They say he might die. He has a family; did you know?"

Hunt looked down. He needed to show remorse. He needed to show how weak and pitiful he was. That he was only trying to survive. Doing what he'd been told.

"He would be with his family if it wasn't for the foreign invaders coming into our lands. You know we have a duty to fight?"

Hunt kept looking down. He felt the man's eyes on him. As if we don't have a duty to fight, Hunt thought.

"We are only trying to do what's best for Afghanistan, you must see that," Abdullah said.

Hunt inferred by this that he was Taliban, not al-Qaeda. That was at least something. He'd heard the Taliban in the *shura* claiming the prisoners. No pissing on his open wounds, just yet.

Hunt lifted his eyes and looked at Lambert. He remained still, but Hunt thought he saw some rapid eye-movement and his shallow breathing meant he was conscious and aware.

Just then Lambert glanced at him to show him that he was alive. The men had a split second of eye contact. His eyes gave so much away. They're the only part of the brain that sticks out of the skull. They tell you when someone is drunk, or lying, when someone is alert, or happy. They were a window into the mind. How much human communication was made with just a look? Hunt even got a small smile out of him. That was all he needed. All it took. Lambert was in there and he was holding on too. Maybe Lambert had seen the fear in Hunt's eyes though, because his partner was in such a bad state. Hunt felt an intense dread for him. Like he might not last.

Lambert dropped his eyes just as swiftly. Hunt looked away from him, so as to be sure that the interrogator wouldn't know that they had 'seen' one another.

"This is what I am prepared to do," Abdullah said. " But,

this offer depends on the man you assaulted, our brother Omar, surviving ... If he survives, the al-Qaeda fighters will not seek your death as revenge for killing him. That was our agreement with them. First, if you cooperate with us, and tell us the things that you know, and the things that we need to know, you will remain in our custody until a deal can be done with the United States."

Hunt shook his head. It was complicated. Hunt didn't think it prudent to mention to him the added complexity of him being British and Lambert being French.

"You can see we are reasonable men. You can see that we are only protecting our homeland and would like some information from you ... In return, as you know, we are not savages. We have provided you with medical attention and we will provide you with food, even as our people suffer due to the sanctions and aggression, we will give to you what little we have. Unlike you, we do not profess to be violent men, but we will be violent in order to defend what is ours. So, if that sounds reasonable?" Abdullah looked at Hunt and waited for a response. When there was none, he continued, and said, "With the formalities out of the way, and taking your silence as agreement, I only have one question for which I need an answer ..."

CHAPTER TWENTY-TWO

Hunt lifted his eyes and narrowed them in anticipation. He didn't want to give anything away. One question. What could it be, he wondered. Would they want to know about the sniper positions? Was he going to be able to give away his colleagues like that? Do they want to know about the defence of Mazar? Or, find out what Lambert and he had reported back to the headquarters? He didn't have long to wait.

"Tell me, *who* in this village assisted you?"

The bottom dropped out of his stomach and he felt his heart rate increase and his cheeks flush. He hadn't expected that. It was a question of precision and subtlety and intricacy. He was asking him to give up the old farmer and the farmer's family. There is no way that the man who helped him would survive past sunset. Hunt and Abdullah both knew it. Hunt saw it in his eyes.

"I'm sorry, I can't answer that question."

Hunt's mentality changed. It was like flipping over a coin. A completely new side. A burst of lightning in a dark sky. The mission wasn't al-Zawahiri for Hunt anymore. How could it be? It was saving Lambert. Saving himself. And saving his friends and the people of Mazar-i-Sharif.

Hunt heard the rumbling thunder in the distance. The Taliban interrogator waited. He watched Hunt and waited for a reaction. Now, more than ever, Hunt was sure the catalyst for the position he found himself in, at that moment, was the act of terrorism that killed his fiancée. Everything had spawned and spilled outwards from that explosion. Did the farmer and his family deserve to be strung up like carcasses in a butcher shop and skinned because they helped a person? Because they followed an ancient code of their people and helped a person who was trying to do the right thing. A person who was fallible. And now, Hunt and his partner were in a terrible, terrible situation.

What had he been through to get here? Was he just going to give it all away to save himself now, after all that? This man, standing in front of him, had no idea of the depths of drive for vengeance he felt. No idea of the lengths he would go to. Hunt sat there, hands strapped behind his back, desperately trying to think of a way out. Had he reached the end of the road?

The thought that al-Zawahiri was going to get away with it gnawed at him like a dog tearing at a juicy bone. It ripped at his insides and thrashed around like some dying thing. Hunt couldn't see a way out. He was trapped. A decision he'd made led to Lambert's capture. They were both likely to be executed. And worse, with no comms and no way out, thousands of fanatical soldiers were already headed towards a badly defended and vulnerable city full of people who only wanted freedom.

As the sharp-nosed, black-eyed man stood there and looked at him, looking into his soul, Hunt realised the full weight of what he'd been through, and that it was just to get to a position of defeat.

All of the physical pain and suffering he'd put his body through. All of the training. All of the nights he'd fallen asleep thinking of the moment when he would finally press the point of a pistol into al-Zawahiri's skull, and pull the trigger.

And now. What did he have ... He was sitting in a stinking, dirty, mud room, in some non-entity of a village, in some mountain range on the edge of the civilised world, and he was going to fail? No. He felt like his mind was playing tricks on him again. Distorting reality. They want you to remove yourself from the pain. They want you to move to a safe space. They don't want you to experience the depths of human despair.

Hunt shook his head involuntarily as the thoughts raced through his brain and the interrogator raised his eyebrows.

"You will tell me ... One way or another. You will tell me."

Hunt knew he was right. Was there a way out? Hunt saw Lambert move his head from side to side very slowly. Almost imperceptibly. He was telling Hunt - screaming at him - don't say *anything*. Lambert was a brave man.

Hunt felt like his decision had put Lambert in this position. But, what choice did he have? Hunt's main driver, his only goal, had been to assassinate al-Zawahiri. And now. Had that changed; could it change?

'Ask me something else ..." Hunt said. "Ask me something else and I will tell you, but I can't tell you that. Just as you profess to follow the honour code, so must I ... And I can't disclose any names to you."

The tall Talib shook his head.

"I am sad," he said. "Fine. Please, just remember that you brought this on yourself ..." He moved over to the planks that made up the door to the interrogation room and banged hard on them once. The door opened and the big, fat, bearded guard was standing there. The interrogator spoke to him and said in Pashto, "I need your help. Come in here and bring your knife. It doesn't matter if it's sharp or not."

"It's not sharp ..." the guard replied.

Hunt swallowed. The big man swayed as he swaggered into the room. He had a bad look in his eye. Hunt wasn't sure what he was feeling at first. As the big man entered, the room suddenly felt small. The walls and the floor and the ceiling were compressing in on him all at once. He felt like a car being crushed by thousands of tons of force. He felt fear. Hunt realised for the first time in years that he was afraid. He anticipated something terrible.

He wasn't sure what. Or maybe he was, but he couldn't admit it to himself. The fat Talib pulled out a long thin blade. The handle was wrapped in some kind of cotton gauze, probably for the sweat that ran down from his armpit, to stop the grip from moving. The blade looked like something you could use as a paring knife. Something for separating vegetables.

Hunt could hear Lambert breathing through his nose, fear pervaded the room like mustard gas. Lambert started to move. His body twitched and his eyes rolled involuntarily. Hunt realised he was trying to get free. He was trying to squeeze his hands free and the intensity in the room grew. Hunt heard the interrogator's voice change. It sounded more high pitched. It sounded like fear had grabbed him by the back of his throat too.

"You will tell me."

"I'm sorry ..."

"There's a savage way and a civilised way -"

"No I won't. You'll have to kill us. Better to die with honour, than live with the shame and guilt."

The screams were unbearable. Hunt felt like pissing his pants and vomiting on the front of his shirt. Lambert cried in agony and in pain.

The big man was standing over Lambert, straddling him. He pulled back on Lambert's head and used the blade to slice at Lambert's face.

"Tell me!" The interrogator screamed over the panic and fear. "Tell me! Tell me! Tell me!"

"Don't tell him, Stirling!" Lambert cried out. The fat man punched him in the mouth. Hunt wasn't sure what he'd done. He wanted to pass out. His brain wanted to recoil. His mind wanted to be somewhere else. He saw flashes of lying on a golden beach with ocean waves rolling up the shore. The image popped in his head and the screams brought him back.

"We've had war for many years! All of our families have suffered. We are not barbarians, you are! It's you who are bringing war. This is a very unfortunate situation for you. Why don't you just help us? Help your friend. Why are you letting him suffer all this pain?"

Hunt could hear the slow, intense grind of the dull blade against Lambert's face. The interrogator tapped the big man on the shoulder and beckoned him away. He wanted Hunt to see the result of his non-compliance.

Hunt looked away and tried to close his eyes tight. Then he felt the big man's hands on his face. They pulled his nose and his eyelids up and twisted his head. He was forced to just stare into the face of his partner. His friend. The person that he'd come to trust. Lambert's face was covered in blood. He had slashes across both his eyes. It looked like the fat man had tried to cut his eyelids off. Lambert was breathing shallow, raspy breaths. He was in excruciating pain. And, through the agony, Lambert said, "*Ne t'avise pas de leur dire une putain de chose*." And spat blood on the floor. Don't tell them a bloody thing.

The interrogator went and slapped Lambert hard with the back of his fist and said, "Shut up!" He pulled his hand back and the white sleeve of his tunic was smeared red with blood. He turned back to Hunt in disgust.

"No, tell me, soldier … Tell me what I want to know and the pain will stop."

Just then, there was a tap on the wooden door. The fat man and the interrogator looked at one another. Abdullah sighed.

"Can you see what they want …" he said to the fat man.

Reluctantly, he released Hunt's face from his thick, strong fingers, and spat on Hunt's face. The fat man went to the door, opened it, and stepped outside. There was a moment of silence. Lambert sobbed a little as blood dripped from the cuts on his face. Hunt felt his own expression change from anguish to anger. Hunt wanted to tell Abdullah, this tormentor, that he was going to die. It would sound ridiculous given the situation. So, he kept it to himself. The fat man opened the door and came back and beckoned the tall man outside, "Come here boss, you need hear this…"

Abdullah hesitated for a moment and glanced at Hunt and then back at the door and outside. He knew he was in the crescendo of the moment, but maybe he felt that a few minutes in silence and in pain staring at a wounded colleague's bloody face might change prisoner's mind. He went out the door and shut it behind him.

Hunt heard the bolt latch, and loud, angry voices outside the door. Someone was shouting. They weren't happy. What was the discussion? Hunt looked at Lambert again and realised that he was looking back at Hunt. Raspy, and under his breath, Lambert said, "Come here. Come here quick. Let me chew your rope."

It was immediately clear what he meant. Hunt was not tied to the chair. He jumped up and hurried over to Lambert. Hunt turned his back and tried to push his arms out, straight behind him. Lambert leaned forward, as far as he could, and Hunt felt his face pressing up against the back of his forearms. Lambert grunted and snorted and whined in pain as he gnawed on the rope that bound Hunt' wrists. He chewed on it as hard as he could manage. Hunt heard his teeth cracking and pulling at it. Lambert tore at the binding like a suffering imbecile. The pain Lambert must've been in, Hunt thought. It made him feel sick. His teeth must be broken, his face must be broken, and now he was getting dirt and grime into those slashes on his face and eyes, but he just suffered and chewed through it. Hunt heard the bolt unlatch.

"Quick, quick, they're coming!" Hunt said in a forceful whisper.

CHAPTER TWENTY-THREE

Hunt pulled his hands away, as he moved them, he felt the rope pull Lambert's teeth and he yelped. Hunt rushed back to the chair. He sat down so fast that it almost broke as he dropped. He was in his seat as the door swung open and a bundle of people pushed in.

Hunt tried his best to see if he could break free. His wrists were looser and he could feel, between finger and thumb, the progress Lambert had made. Hunt started rubbing furiously between his thumbnail and the rope to try and cut some of the fibres enough that he could break his wrists free.

The men who burst into the room filled the space and they were still arguing. They shouted at one another gesturing with open palms first at Hunt and then at the interrogator and then at themselves. They were expressive and agitated. Something had happened. Hunt was trying to think at the same time as he was trying to free his wrists.

He was also trying to calculate what he would do when his wrists were freed. Sacrifice himself and save Lambert? Would he be able to disarm and otherwise debilitate five Taliban and al-Qaeda terrorists standing in the room with his bare hands? He'd have to relieve Abdullah of the service pistol in his waistband.

In amongst the rabble and infighting, the interrogator stepped forward. His white robe and red sleeve and white, wrapped head contrasted him against the black turbans and camouflage jackets of the al-Qaeda fighters. He was very much the local politician, while they were not. He raised his palms towards them and the hubbub died down. He looked directly at Hunt and said, "These men have found the bodies."

At first, Hunt wasn't sure what he meant. Then it quickly dawned on him. Found the bodies of their comrades. They found the bodies of the fellow Islamic students Hunt had sent off to their heaven. The one under the tarp and shrubbery that he'd choked to death, or, perhaps something else had happened.

"The man you're attacked next to the alley," Abdullah said. "He has died. In your shameful wickedness, you have killed our brother, Omar. This man was a leader for them, and his loss will be felt very deeply. These men are here to thank you. Our agreement was to give you some hours to confess, but that is now broken. Now, you will be executed like a common criminal. They will make an example of you for your colleagues. For your comrades. For your fellow soldiers. And, for the world."

Big responsibility, Hunt thought. What did 'make an example of' actually mean? Abdullah continued, "These men will take you now."

Hunt panicked as they grabbed him. "Am I not entitled to a trial?" Hunt asked. He tried to hide the desperation in his voice. "We're not entitled to a defence, for my actions? Am I not entitled to some protection under the Geneva Convention?"

"But, we are not at war," Abdullah said as they lifted Hunt up and dragged him out. Abdullah was very serious and he shouted after Hunt, "You and your government may think we are at war, but you are an invader in an independent country! We are merely defending our soil. You are attacking us. No convention can save you!"

"So no trial, no free trial. No ability to speak for myself?"

"That is not how things work in this land. You have been found guilty by the elders and you must pay a price for your sedition. We have given your punishment over to our brothers in the struggle. No, they will decide what to do to make an example of you."

Now Hunt knew what 'an example' meant. He'd heard the stories from people who'd found captured soldiers before. That was where the advice to blow his brains out, before they could string him up and piss on his open wounds, came from. As they grabbed and pulled him, a few gave him some punches and elbows to his head.

They knocked him around as they dragged him out into the streets. There was a small crowd of the few fighters that had remained in the village, and some elderly people from the village itself. His captors announced proudly, "This is the traitor! This is the murderer! *Insha'Allah*, we will have our justice, and the infidel will see that they are making a mistake thinking that they can come here and impose themselves!"

The crowd were appreciative and cheered and showed their vitriolic hatred and anger towards Hunt. He was afraid again. Now he truly didn't know what was going to happen. Lambert was a dead man, and he'd be strung up by his skin as a warning to the west. No one was coming for them. He knew it. Hunt doubted they even knew where he was, or what had happened to them. They were truly alone and at the mercy of this tribe of people living in conditions from the Middle Ages. People from the Middle Ages who'd maintained the same hard and violent and merciless way of life for thousands of years.

CHAPTER TWENTY-FOUR

It sounded to Hunt like he was going to be a warning to others. The terrorists with their fragile egos and paranoid fear of America meant they were lashing out. Trying to make the enemy submit through sheer terror at the foe they were facing. They were going to publicly execute him. The full show.

Hunt was happy to be a cautionary tale. But, he wasn't going to go down in the supplicated manner they were hoping for. He had to try and get the attention of the other snipers in overwatch over the other villages, and hope that they saw the activity, and reported it. Maybe headquarters would act on it and send a satellite or drone to check it out. Hunt had heard that they'd used a drone in the first targeted assassination a few months before. It had failed colossally.

He also wouldn't have minded hearing the thunderous turbines of some 'Angel of Death' AC-130 Spectre gunships coming over the mountains. Hunt tried to resist as they carried him out. He managed to contort into a position that pulled against the guys carrying him. He thought he was going to snap his wrists as he twisted against their force. He bit down on his back molars, tensed his muscles, and twisted his body, it looked like someone breaking dried spaghetti in half. Lambert had gnawed part of the way through the rope.

The force Hunt exerted snapped it and he felt his muscles suddenly release and the pressure in the back of his jaw relax. As he felt it snap, he immediately jumped on one of the guards. Hunt got behind him and squashed his neck under his forearm in a choke and went to grab the AK-47 slung on the guard's front. Hunt got the rifle off him and fired wildly into the crowd of Taliban and al-Qaeda soldiers on the street. Some fell where they'd stood as the bullets tore into their soft, unprotected chests and lungs.

The crowd scattered. Some of the braver soldiers lifted their AK-47 rifles, looked for cover, and tried to return fire. Hunt had no idea what he was going to do, he just knew that he was going down fighting. No matter what. He yelled a violent, deep-throated war cry in a jumbled mix of English and Shona. His language from Rhodesia.

Hunt still had the terrorist pinned against his body as a human shield. The guy put his arms up and around the back of Hunt's head and pulled his face into his shoulder.

Hunt tried to resist, but the man squeezed like his life depended on it. It did. Hunt's finger was still on the AK-47 trigger and the weapon blasted a wild spray of bullets into mud walls and the hard dust and rounds ricocheted around him. The mechanism *clack-clack-clacked* and all of a sudden it froze. Oh, no. Not now. Stoppage!

Seconds later, Hunt felt hands grab him and pull him down to the ground and hold him there. They were all jabbering and shouting. They got behind him and sat on his legs and back to stop him from moving.

"No! You bastards! No!" He tried to fight them off. His face was in the dirt and his cheek pressed hard against the compacted dust. The last thing he saw was the sole of a brown boot coming at his face. The blow knocked him out.

WHEN HE CAME TO, HE WAS LYING ON A MOUND OF DIRT, to the south of the village. He lifted his head off the dirt to get his bearings. To his right in the distance he could see the old farmer's homestead.

The al-Qaeda commander was addressing a small crowd that had gathered at the base of the mound for the spectacle. Hunt saw a few younger guys holding hand-held video cameras. He was going to be the top of the international news hour.

The crowd looked mostly like it was members of the village and some of the more elderly Taliban. There were a handful of al-Qaeda-looking soldiers in their military jackets and black turbans and they death-stared Hunt and bit their thumbs at him and spat in his direction. They were angry. Good.

The main cohort of fighters had obviously left, as he'd suspected from the conversation he'd overheard between the guards and Abdullah. Hunt's wrists were each tied with a length of rope. Each rope was held by an al-Qaeda guard, standing on either side of him. They flanked him. Each held the rope in one hand and had the other on an AK-47. They yanked on the ropes when they saw he was awake and pulled him to his knees.

As Hunt knelt on the mound he looked out at the meagre crowd. He was a bit disappointed. If he was going to be made a spectacle of he would've preferred there to at least be more interest.

He wished more people cared about whether he lived or

died. Maybe it was just selfishness and vanity to think like that.

As the man addressed the crowd Hunt realised he was only standing on one leg. He had a crutch under his right arm. As he turned to look back at Hunt, he saw that without doubt the man was Mullah Dadullah. The man who'd originally led the Taliban and al-Qaeda forces into the 'valley of the four villages' and put them within attacking distance of Mazar-i-Sharif. This was the man they'd been sent to find.

And now, he was the man who was going to execute them. Hunt saw a pile of planks of wood next to the mound. Some of the al-Qaeda soldiers were working on building something with hammers and nails. There was more twine in a small pile and some soldiers behind him were digging a hole in the mound.

Was it to be his grave? Surely they wouldn't bury him on this mound. Dadullah said, "Al-Qaeda will institute an old punishment to execute this infidel who brutally assaulted and killed our brothers. He has been tried by the council and found guilty of murder. Enemies of this land, and all peoples, must know: we, the ruling Taliban, will be re-implementing the ancient punishment of crucifixion. This enemy of God will hang here in the sun with his wounds open for the vultures and the buzzards, *insha'Allah*, to come and pick at his flesh and pull out his eyes, until finally he succumbs in shame for his sin."

The al-Qaeda fighters in the crowd cheered and started a chant and warble like native Americans. The villagers were less enthused and a few reluctantly joined in the clapping and the chanting. Dadullah raised his arms and gave the order to the soldiers working on the wood to bring the cross and they carried it behind him.

THERE WAS NO WAY HUNT WAS GOING TO LET THIS HAPPEN. Not like they wanted it to. Even though it aligned with needing to send a message, this wasn't exactly the message he wanted to send. He drove a fist into the side of the knee of the guard standing to his right. There was a commotion on top of the mound and Dadullah yelled and twisted on his leg and slipped on the edge of the slope. Hunt was flailing wildly and aggressively. Big hooks smashed into the body and head of the guard who'd fallen on his back. Hunt was tackled to the ground from behind, the guard got on top of him, and pulled his tunic up so it covered his head like a bag. He couldn't see. Hunt felt the butt of a rifle biting into his head and body as he struggled. They hit him over and over.

As he twisted to get away he felt the rifle come down hard on the back of his head and his vision popped and was filled with exploding bubbles and a bright light. The pain was excruciating and intense.

He came to once again and wanted to rub the lump and pain on the side of his head. He moved to touch it and his arm pulled tight against a rope. He lay on his side with a rough-hewn piece of timber plank running the length of his arm behind him.

One of the guards held a nail to Hunt's palm and another had a sledgehammer in his hands. They were about to nail him to a cross. This was a nightmare. His mind backed away from him as it recoiled. This couldn't be happening. It can't.

Hunt had other men holding him down and he struggled and tried to move away, but they pinned him. The man on his knees lifted the hammer. He held it right above where above the metal stake was being held against the palm of his open hand. The hammer fell and there was a searing white-hot heat. Hunt saw the nail driven through his skin, into the nerve endings and bone of his right hand. He screamed out. He didn't want to. He couldn't help it. The pain was unreal.

It was the most intense pain he'd ever felt. Just before the blow fell again and the metal sledgehammer struck the nail again. There was a *hiss* and a *snap* of bullets as they were fired over Hunt's head. Then he heard the *clap-clap-clap-clap* of automatic fire and someone yelling from a distance in Pashto.

Hunt heard the *clap-clap-clap* again and rounds slammed into the body of the man on his knees about to hammer Hunt's hand to the plank of wood. The hammer fell from the guy's grip and Hunt saw blood coming out of the wounds in his torso. Tosser.

The guy looked down and raised his hands to touch the blood with a disbelieving expression on his face. His body flopped to the ground. His corpse would be wearing that look of surprise forever.

There was a commotion of people running and screaming and the small crowd dispersed. Mullah Dadullah was screaming and pointing towards the farmer's fields. The men around him reacted and jumped away to find some cover. Hunt had no idea what was going on. An assault? Had they found him?

It didn't matter. He needed to get up and get away. Hunt scrambled to his knees. He yanked and tried to pull the nail out but it wouldn't budge. It hurt like hell. He grabbed the nail with his left hand and tried to wiggle it. He felt the rusted nail rasp against the bones between his fingers and his brain screamed out in pain and blood seeped out of his palm.

Hunt yelled out. A deep roar of grunting pain and agony and hate and fear and used his left hand to squeeze tight against the nail in his right and wiggled it. Hunt screamed and then laughed as it broke free. It was relief. Pure ecstasy. He turned to see Mullah Dadullah scrambling down the side of the mound as the bullets *cracked* and *snapped* overhead.

Hunt didn't care about them. He held the dripping bloody nail in his functional left hand.

He looked across and saw the old farmer carrying Hunt's rifle. The Minimi that he'd left at the farmer's house. The farmer fired it at the mound. He was shouting something. "He's my guest! My honour! We have a duty as a nation! I have a responsibility! Do not kill him!"

The old farmer had come to his rescue. Hunt was his guest, no matter what, this man was bound by his culture and his religion to protect him.

Mullah Dadullah slid down the side of the mound on his stomach and pulled himself along with his hands and pushed himself forward with his one good leg.

Hunt immediately went for him. He brought up the rusted nail clenched in his fist. He moved towards Dadullah like a dog chasing a cat. Hunt got on top of him and the man screamed out. Hunt brought the nail down on the back of his head and neck.

Dadullah screamed in pain and tried to turn over, but Hunt made a fist in his bloody, bleeding right hand and pounded it into the one-legged Talib's face head over and over. He punched with arching hooks like a heavyweight would a punching bag. The nail drove home with every left he threw. It sounded like he was slapping meat, except for the screams.

Hunt brought the nail down onto Dadullah's cheek and neck and as he did the old farmer ran up to him, out of breath and totally exhausted. Hunt turned, and the farmer heaved and said: "Here! Take it," and thrust the Minimi into Hunt's chest.

Hunt took it while on his knees and checked the weapon and brought it to bear. Dadullah writhed on the ground and clutched at his head and neck. He gurgled as blood came out of his mouth. Hunt stood over him. He didn't have anything clever to say. He fired two rounds into the chest and one into the head. Double tap, single tap. The Taliban leader stopped moving. Hunt reached down and grabbed the ICOM radio from Dadullah's body. He had the Taliban comms network now.

Hunt scurried up the mound and fired onto the al-Qaeda soldiers crouched and hiding behind it for cover. The automatic rounds tore through them and the bodies fell. The farmer grabbed Hunt by the robe and tried to pull him down and away. Hunt didn't care if he died. His chest heaved. Blood seeped out of his wounds. He stood on the mound looking at the death below him.

The farmer was yelling at him as he pulled him out of harm's way, "We must go! We must go! You need to leave!"

Hunt knew what he had to do.

CHAPTER TWENTY-FIVE

No one was coming to help them. Hunt realised that he and Lambert were on their own. His actions had added to the stalemate. He'd brought it upon himself by pursuing his personal revenge mission. And, the fallout had swept up people not connected with his desire. Now, he realised, he needed to get help. He needed to make up for his mistake. One thing was for certain, he was going to do everything in his power to fix it. He would put it right one way or another. Lambert deserved it and God knew the old farmer deserved it.

Hunt took off at a run. Bullets from al-Qaeda fighters *hissed* and *snapped* overhead as he put distance between himself and the village. He bobbed and weaved and used the undulating ground as cover. He headed back to the compound. He had a plan which included making enough of a noise that someone would *have to* hear it.

As he ran, Hunt pressed the ICOM radio pressell and yelled into the receiver: "This is Captain Stirling Hunt. Call sign bravo-six-zero. I repeat, bravo-six-zero. We are compromised! Request immediate QRF evac. Location: south of

Yawur village. One soldier captured. Lambert is captured! Request immediate QRF support! Grid: three-six-two-one, six-nine-five-three. Grid: three-six-two-one, six-nine-five-three. I repeat require media QRF support!"

The message was a bit jumbled, but they'd get the idea. He said the grid twice as per standard operating procedure. Hunt had no idea if anyone would hear him. He knew that the other al-Qaeda and Taliban fighters would have heard the transmission. He didn't know if someone was manning the Delta Force desk on the top floor of the Old Turkish Schoolhouse, like he had before the mission. He could only hope that somebody in the CIA was doing their job listening in on the scanners and heard his cries for help. He limped on, running breathless back to the farmer's homestead.

Hunt burst through the gate that led to the farmer's compound and ran straight into the house. No time for manners now. The children ran to their mother and Hunt tried to apologise, but he was in a rush.

He went to his kit in the corner of the living room and threw off the traditional Pashtun robes. He pulled on his body armour and smock and strapped his webbing around his hips and pulled the nylon strap tight and put his rucksack on. He reloaded the Minimi, and looked up at the wife as he wrapped his wounded hand in gauze.

"Where are the keys?" he said too forcefully in Pashto.

She stared at him blankly, her eyes wide with fear.

"Where are the keys to the ..."

Hunt didn't know the word for tractor, so he mimicked turning the engine over and the rumble and roar of the tractor engine with his lips. The children were afraid, but they laughed at the game.

He sounded like a grizzly bear trying to ward off some intruder. He held the imaginary tractor steering wheel and Hunt pressed the accelerator. Suddenly the old farmer's wife clicked and realised what he was trying to say and pointed to the single hook on the wall at the entrance.

"Thank you," Hunt said and walked over to the keys on the wall. He snatched them and went out to the courtyard and climbed aboard the tractor. Hunt had seen the farmer clearing ditches and removing unwanted debris from his land. Now, Hunt just had to think back to his younger days on the farm in Rhodesia and remember how to drive it. He used to know these old tractors well. They were very simple and reliable. Everything he wished to be. He fired it up and black smoke puffed out of the upright exhaust pipe.

CHAPTER TWENTY-SIX

Hunt ground the gears as he fiddled with the clutch trying to get it to bite. The engine growled at him. Then the tractor lurched forward and jolted and Hunt rocked on the seat.

"Now we're talking ..." he said.

He set the tractor on the path towards the village and once he'd lined it up, facing the village, he came to a halt. He fiddled with the levers again until the bucket attachment on the front raised up. When it was as high as it could go, he tilted it so that the bottom teeth were flat against the lever. He positioned it so that it protected him from the front in the driver's seat, like a shield.

Next, he took out his emergency locator beacon and switched it on. He wasn't sure how reliable or accurate it was, but they'd been told that the signal would be picked up by satellite and that it was accurate to within seventy feet of his actual position. Hunt had no idea if anyone was listening, or looking out for them, but he hoped.

He had to try. Even if he failed. He ground the tractor's gears again and it pulled forward with a lurch. Hunt kept talking into the ICOM radio.

He repeated his name, rank, number and his approximate position to eight grid squares. If anybody heard him on the ICOM chatter monitoring, they *had to* put two and two together and send the quick reaction force, surely? As it was, the tractor moved forward and Hunt saw the old farmer coming towards him. The farmer lifted his hand to his brow to protect his eyes from the sun and he looked up at Hunt in the driver's seat. Hunt said, "Thank you, my friend! Thank you more than you can ever know."

Hunt bounced and jolted in the driver's seat towards the village at full pace. It would be difficult to fire accurately from the sitting position. As he drove north towards the village, he saw the mound where he'd nearly been crucified. His hand was still bleeding and he pumped his fingers by making a fist to try and stop the muscles from seizing up.

He was almost within range of the village now. He stopped the tractor and put it in neutral. He climbed down from the driver's seat and lifted his weapon and scanned the area. He couldn't see anything. He opened the side of the tractor's engine cover and it folded up. He found the accelerator cable and gave it a pull and the engine roared as the cylinders fired faster. He left it open so that there was power applied to the engine without him pressing the accelerator.

Then he went back to the controls. Hunt put his rucksack under the steering wheel to keep it level and straight. He put it in gear and the tractor lurched forward. The tractor trundled up the main road where the market was, and headed towards the mosque in the centre of the town.

Hunt walked alongside the tractor as a soldier walked beside a tank. He used the vehicle for cover and kept an eye out for sharpshooters from the windows and murder holes and alleyways that lined the main drag. The tactic had been employed since the Germans invaded cities in Europe and was still practiced by armoured corps' soldiers.

He manoeuvred forward into the village and used the tractor as a base of fire. As he walked behind it, he swivelled on his heels and moved into different positions to try and defend himself. He felt like he was walking into a swarm of bees. He just didn't know where they were.

The village had multiple prime firing points looking down onto the main road, it was the alleyways and compound walls along the route that Hunt feared, where bandits could pop out and have a go.

There were also the cinder block-sized holes in the sides of walls and in the sides of houses. They were called murder holes. Sharpshooters could fire statically, safely and unseen.

Hunt only had one thing on his mind. He had to get to Lambert and pull him out of there, even if it was the last thing he did with his life. He saw movement over to his left. An enemy fighter came out of a narrow alleyway. It was the same alley Hunt had been caught in only hours before.

The man's face showed surprise when he saw the tractor, but quickly switched to a mixture of fear and panic as he saw Hunt swivel with the Minimi. As the enemy fighter raised his AK-47, Hunt gave a quick squeeze on the trigger and riddled his enemy with bullets. They ripped his clothes apart and smacked into the mud walls around him.

The quick fire drew attention, and Hunt heard shouts and activity. These weren't the shouts of confident men though.

These were the shouts of men who'd just seen one of their close colleagues slaughtered on the street, their leader's head and neck pummelled with the nail meant for the prisoner, and the bodies of their colleagues piling up in the compounds. They'd soon start to smell. Hunt kept moving forward with the tractor.

Occasionally he'd walk to the cockpit and adjust the steering slightly to keep it going straight towards the mosque. Those were dangerous moments. Between the Taliban and al-Qaeda, they hadn't left many fighters. All the best men would have moved north, before they would turn west, to attack Mazar-i-Sharif.

They were committed and fundamentalist, but none of them was more committed and single-minded than the man they were attacking. Hunt knew it. He'd decided he wasn't going to lose.

Hunt saw more gun barrels poke out from murder holes overlooking the road. He fired on the positions. Mud and wood flaked and spun off the walls as the rounds slammed into the sides of the buildings. Hunt moved forward, protected by the tractor all the while. Sometimes he took a knee to fire and then ran to catch up. Men started appearing from everywhere.

They jumped out in front of the tractor and fired wildly and then ran back behind cover. Hunt never saw one of them aim their weapons once. AK-47s appeared over walls held there by a hand and an invisible body. Rounds pinged and bounced off the old tractor. They seemed to be coming from everywhere. Hunt swore at himself as he involuntarily ducked his head. He *had to* keep it up, despite the incoming rounds, to see where they were coming from and try and return fire.

Hunt took cover as the 7.62 rounds sprayed all around him and slammed into the sides and front of the tractor. The sound of metallic grating and clanging rang out like a black-smith's hammer hitting an anvil.

He had a quick check around the large rubber rear tyre. He couldn't be more than three hundred yards from the mosque wall. He reloaded quickly while he was in a crouch.

When he looked up, he saw a Talib jump hurriedly out and stand in the road in front of the tractor. Oh, God, he's got an RPG. Hunt was about to dive behind the tractor to take cover. Something flicked in his mind. It wasn't even a decision. His nervous system simply reacted. Instead of diving sideways, he half turned to his left and dove forward.

The tractor moved forward to his front right. He was prone with the automatic rifle in front of him. He put his eyes behind the optical sight and saw the Talib ready to fire the rocket propelled grenade.

It could go anywhere. These guys had no formal training. *Insha'Allah*. Yeah. Let's see how much your God cares for you ... Hunt pulled back on the trigger and held it for an internal count of *one-one-thousand*.

Dust flew up in front of the rifle as the ten rounds found their target. They sliced through the Talib and knocked him backwards. The guy fell backwards and the rocket ignited. The unmistakable *hiss* and *pop* as the grenade left the launcher. Now Hunt dived for cover.

He ducked his chin and rolled to his right. Men screamed from behind a wall to his left. A trail of smoke followed the grenade as it zipped and spiralled over the wall and into the side of a second floor.

It exploded with the ferocity and sickening blast that grabbed you at the base of the throat. The compound with the pale-blue, solid metal gate was coming up on his right. The tractor was about to drive past it and crush the Talib who'd just been filled with lead and steel bullets.

CHAPTER TWENTY-SEVEN

CHANGE OF PLANS. Hunt ran up to the steering wheel. He grabbed it and pulled on it and launched himself up and into the driver's seat. A bullet *snapped* over his head. He ducked involuntarily and swore at himself again for reacting. This was no time for nerves. He jammed the steering wheel hard right and pressed his foot into the accelerator. The tractor lurched and sped momentarily before it smashed into the compound wall. Hunt got up and crouched on the driver's seat. He saw some heads poking up above the compounds across the street. He pulled two smoke grenades from his webbing and dropped them behind the tractor.

They hissed and spun in the dust and wafted thick plumes of white smoke as cover. Smoke was always a double-edged sword, because the smoke attracted fire, but Hunt just hoped that the unaimed bullets would miss. He lifted the Minimi and emptied a magazine into the wall opposite. In his head he counted *one, two, three* and turned and ran up the tractor's front, put one foot on the bucket attachment, which had buried itself into the mud wall, his other foot was on top of the compound wall. His quadricep and gluteal muscles exploded and he leaped down into the space below.

Hunt landed with a heavy thud in a crouch; with one knee and one fist on the ground, rifle cradled under his forearm and trapped under his armpit. Bullets slammed into the roof and side of the building above him. The thick smoke billowed over the top of the compound wall. Men ran at him. He used the rifle as a club. He lifted it and drove it into the face of the fanatic to his front. His vision was narrowed. Fear is a powerful drug. The brain reacts by releasing large amounts of dopamine. Time slowed down for him. He saw everything clearly and with clarity, like a boxer ducking punches in the ring.

The adrenaline in his blood made his reactions seem automatic. He didn't really hear anything and, if he did, it sounded like someone shouting underwater. The sweet stench of smoke stung his nostrils. He pushed the weapon upwards and the man fell back and Hunt drove him into the ground. He got on top of the guy. The guy's head writhed from side to side. He was screaming but the din in Hunt's ears covered the sound.

Hunt's eyes were wide. Crazed. His teeth were firmly clenched. He let go of the Minimi and reached behind his back. He felt the top of his webbing and grabbed the handle of his Royal Marine Fairbairn–Sykes fighting knife. He put his left hand on the man's forehead and pinned it down. He brought the blade down in a low swoop and jammed it into the side of his enemy's neck. Kill, or be killed. He repeated the blows until the neck was punctured five times. Just enough that the enemy was disabled. Hunt climbed off him, wiped the blade on his trousers, and put the bloodstained blade between his teeth and picked up the Minimi.

There were harried and angry shouts coming from inside the main building. Hunt reloaded and pulled the charging handle. He put the knife back in its sheath and wiped the taste from around his mouth and spat. Hunt heard banging on the compound door. Men trying to get in. He looked at the entrance to the building and said, "Bugger it."

He pulled out a grenade and pulled the pin. He lobbed it over the wall and it landed just in front of the pale-blue gate. He turned and heard the screams of panic. He lifted the rifle and pinned the butt into the centre of his chest. There was the violent and grotesque blast from the grenade and the screaming of wounded men. He flinched and swore at himself again and moved into the dim dankness of the building.

Hunt could still smell the smoke. It gave everything a misty haze. He was suddenly aware of his deep breathing and racing heart. He was tired. He took a long inhale and sighed. Nearly there. Then Hunt saw him. The fat man who'd cut Lambert's face. When the fat man saw Hunt he tried to get into the interrogation room. Hunt charged forward. The man squealed and jostled with the latch. Too late. Hunt stopped, rifle raised, pointing at his target. He had the fat terrorist torturer in the graticule. He fired a burst and the rounds *thwapped* into their target.

The fat man made grunting noises as he slid down the wall and onto the floor. He went to lift his AK-47. Hunt walked up to him and stepped on it. Blood seeped out of the torturer's wounds. Hunt was crazed and angry and he fired into the figure on the floor before him. It went limp. He heard something behind him and three men rushed into the passage. They struggled with one another, first to lift their weapons, then when they saw Hunt bring his rifle to bear, they scrambled to get away. Hunt fired and they fell in a congealed pile of contorted bodies. One of them screamed and tried to crawl away. He was pinned.

Hunt heard something behind the latched door that the dead fat man was lying in front of. He stepped to the side, away from the door, and bullets hit the wooden door from the inside and chips flew. Hunt twisted his face away and closed his eyes. The firing stopped. He took three quick deep breaths and rammed his shoulder into the door. The latch popped and he burst into the room. The white bearded man was standing in front of him holding Hunt's Glock. Abdullah. The interrogator. He backed away and lifted his rifle again. Hunt roared like a silverback and charged him. He stuck the barrel of the SAW in the skin under Abdullah's chin. The barrel pushed through his beard and the man fell backwards, "No! No! Please!" he yelled.

Time to meet your maker. Give him my regards. I'll see him soon enough. Hunt pulled on the trigger and the automatic rifle kicked and bucked like a bronco. He roared above the exploding rounds as he emptied the magazine. Bullets tore into their target. The smell of burning flesh and cordite was strangely comforting. He was doing his job. He kept on. The rounds had nearly cut the torturer's head clean off his neck. The gun stopped firing. Hunt wiped his brow. It was filmed with sweat and he stepped back from the corpse. He pulled his hand away from his forehead and it was streaked with blood and dirt. Lambert was sitting there in the same chair just looking at him.

"Alright mate?" Hunt said through deep breaths. He wanted to retch. He had a pit in his stomach. He stank. Lambert's face was full of cuts and the blood was congealed. Hunt slung the Minimi and took his fighting knife and cut Lambert free. Lambert's hands immediately went to his face.

"Don't touch it! Wait, here ..." Hunt went around and crouched in front of him and put his left hand on Lambert's forehead. He moaned in pain and sat backwards like he was waiting for the barber.

"You came back for me ..." Lambert said though swollen lips and broken teeth. He was choked up. Almost in tears. "I would cry right now if it wouldn't bloody sting so much!" he said and tried to laugh. It came out more like he was afraid. Hunt didn't blame him.

Hunt took the emergency medical kit from his webbing and said, "It's good to see you too, partner," and doused a bandage in iodine and wiped Lambert's face. "You might experience a transient burning sensation," Hunt said and choked up a little at the thought of it.

Lambert inhaled sharply at the sting. "Hold on, nearly there ..." Hunt said and stood to bandage the wounds. He went over Lambert's left eye and he stopped Hunt with his hands and said, "No, not this one. I can still see out of this one."

Hunt bandaged the rest of his head and tied it off. He'd left Lambert's left eye free and clear. Even though it was cut across the brow, it wasn't as deep as the right side, and Hunt could see his eyeball was intact. Hunt heard voices from down the corridor. They'd broken into the compound.

"Now what?" Lambert asked him.

"Good question. Let's get the hell out of here."

He pulled Lambert up and they stood. He groaned. His ribs were broken and he held his arm across his chest.

"Can you move?"

Lambert nodded and said, "*Oui*."

Hunt grabbed the handgun from the bloodied corpse of the man who used to be called Abdullah, but was now just a headless, faceless pile of bloodied human meat.

"Prick," Hunt said as he lifted the Glock out of his grip. He checked the magazine and loaded it and said, "Here," and handed it to Lambert. Lambert nodded his thanks. "Guard the door," Hunt said and went to lift the Minimi. The barrel was covered in bits of skin and blood. The smell of human barbecue and cordite was strong.

Hunt reached into his webbing and pulled out the emergency locator beacon. "What's that?" Lambert said and Hunt glanced at him to see him crouched at the door in a firing position, but looking at Hunt.

"*ELT*," Hunt said, "Emergency locator transmitter," and put it on the window ledge. He turned back to Lambert and shrugged. "Maybe they'll get the transmission."

"Maybe they won't," Lambert said.

"Yeah," Hunt said and reloaded the Minimi. "But no need to be so optimistic about it, bloody Frenchman." He glanced at Lambert with a wry grin. "Last magazine," Hunt said.

Just then Lambert turned and fired suddenly. A Talib fell in the passageway in the entrance of the interrogation room.

"Screw it," Hunt said. "I've got an idea. Cover me."

Lambert leaned out and put precious rounds of covering fire down the corridor. There was scrambling sounds and shouts. Hunt ducked out and pulled the body of the fallen Talib in front of the doorway and on top of the fat man. He piled the dead bodies like they were sandbags and then stepped back. Lambert moved and he closed the door and tried to lock it from the inside. He dragged the chairs over and pinned them up against the wood and used Abdullah's corpse as a wedge.

Hunt stood there, chest heaving, after the exertion.

"Brew?" he asked Lambert with a grin and the Legionnaire just death stared him with his one working eye from under the wrapped bandage and said, "*Putain d'anglais, comment peux-tu avoir de l'humour à un moment comme celui-ci.*" How can you laugh at a time like this.

Hunt shrugged and said, "Could be worse."

CHAPTER TWENTY-EIGHT

THEY HUNKERED DOWN. After some time they heard voices and activity outside. Their enemy was getting their confidence back after the onslaught. Hunt was worried. They were low on ammunition and low on morale. The light was fading. It was dusk and soon it would be dark. It was getting cold as their wet-with-sweat clothes stuck to them and their bodies cooled. Just then a rock came through the window and a head popped up and looked into the room. Hunt blasted the glass with a burst of automatic fire.

"*Merde*!" Lambert shouted as the noise from the gun cleared. He was covering his ears. Hunt's ears rang like a dinner bell and then settled into a high-pitched shrill whine. The echo and percussion in the mud-walled room was debilitating. When he fired indoors he could feel the pressure in the room change with the power from the weapon. Just then something else came flying in through the window. It hit the back wall and spun around on the hard floor.

"Grenade!" Lambert shouted and dived for it. As he was in the air, before he reached it, Hunt snatched it up off the floor, twisted, stood on his tip-toes, and posted it back through the window. They heard it thud. They both crouched and covered their ears. Another horrendous blast. And more screaming. Hunt always felt like he'd been kicked in the gut because of the excruciatingly low frequency of a grenade blast. They were as demoralising as they were dangerous. The screaming continued from outside the window. Shrapnel from the grenade had torn into someone's body and they were lying there now and seriously considering their life choices. Hunt heard people pulling the body away and then voices outside the door. Their heads cocked to listen. Scraping and clattering. They were trying to move the bodies, he thought.

"They're trying to move the bodies!" Hunt yelled. Lambert moved forward and grabbed the latch. Hunt kneeled just off centre of the doorway and gave Lambert a nod. The Frenchman closed his eyes tight and dropped his head and said, "*Un, deux, trois,*" and pulled the door open. Hunt saw the wide eyes and surprised face of a bearded al-Qaeda fanatic in front of him. The man froze. He was holding onto the dead fat man's arm.

"I'm not quite finished with that," Hunt said and squeezed. The terrorist's body spun and twisted and fell face first and arse up against the wall. Hunt jumped up and moved forward. He met another al-Qaeda fighter as he was about to step out. This guy had his AK-47 raised, but instead of firing he nearly jumped out of his skin in fright at the sight of Hunt, who looked like a blood-covered grizzly with a gun, coming at him. The SAW cut him in half and he fell widthways across the passage and blocked it. Hunt heard footsteps running away as other fighters retreated. He stepped back into the room and lowered his weapon. His chest was heaving again.

"Hard bloody work this," he said and felt lightheaded. He knew he and Lambert couldn't keep this up forever. Hell, maybe not even for another hour. Lambert shut the door behind him and they dragged Abdullah back to his position as wedge. Hunt took some deep breaths and eyed up Lambert. The Frenchman was clearly in pain. They were tired, hurt, hungry, and thirsty. They hadn't slept in days. They had dozens of Taliban and al-Qaeda warriors trying to get them and no idea if help would arrive before they were overwhelmed. Lambert checked his weapon and Hunt did the same. They still had the fat man's AK-47, but that was it. At least their bodies had enough adrenaline for several lifetimes.

"We can't stay here," Hunt said.

"Where can we go?" Lambert asked and sank on his haunches against the wall. They both listened. There was more noise and activity outside.

"I don't know. Head out of the village? There's a tractor outside I might be able to start it."

"A tractor?"

"Yeah, a red one."

"Cool," Lambert said. "I don't think that will work though."

"What is that?" Hunt said. There was some kind of noise. A hissing sound. The smell of benzene hit them. Diesel. It stank. A yellow plastic container appeared at the window and knocked the emergency transmitter off the ledge as it pushed its way in. The fuel ran over the windowsill and down the wall. Lambert raised his Glock and fired at the hands holding the container. There was a yell and it dropped. Hunt heard a lighter flick open and then a torch on a stick appeared.

"They're trying to smoke us out," Hunt said. The flashpoint of diesel was much higher than for petrol, so it took longer to light it. That gave them time. There were excited shouts and whoops outside and Hunt pulled out his last grenade. He pulled the pin and got on tiptoes and posted it through the window. He heard shouts and scampering and then the grenade detonated. The high pitched ringing in his ears continued. He'd been too late. Flames shot up on the outside of the window and then appeared inside along the wall and the floor. The glow was strong and orange in the dark room against the dark sky.

"Come on, we've got to go," Hunt said and pulled Lambert to his feet and he moved the dead body from the door. Just then there was a sloshing outside the window and they turned to see the yellow fuel container had reappeared. This time it had a rag sticking out the top of it. They held it in the flames and it caught alight.

"Come on!" Hunt yelled and pulled open the door. As he did the yellow container came into the room and fell with a heavy thud onto the interrogation room floor. Hunt and Lambert stepped over the dead bodies. They exited in a hurry and turned left, and ran deeper into the maze of the compound. Hunt twisted and saw shapes and figures moving at the far end of the corridor, back towards the entrance. He fired a few bursts down the dark passage as they ran. Lambert coughed. The smell of burning diesel and smoke filled the passage. They both coughed. Hunt bundled Lambert to the end of the passage and they both collapsed against the wall. They were trapped. Fire and Taliban soldiers blocked their escape. Hunt took the Glock from Lambert and checked the magazine.

"What're you doing?" Lambert said. "Give it back."

"Just making sure we have enough bullets to blow our brains out, if it comes to it," Hunt said and slapped the weapon back into Lambert's outstretched palm. They heard a sound far away. Dull and distant at first. Coming closer. Growing. It turned into a pulse, like the hum of an amplifier that was placed too close to a speaker.

CHAPTER TWENTY-NINE

Helicopters. Not just any helicopters. U.S. Army Chinook MH-47E Nightstalker helicopters. The quick reaction force was inbound. A night raid.

"They've come for us!" Lambert shouted over the noise as the choppers buzzed over the village. Hunt heard them move south to land on the open land near the old farmer's field. The smoke was still spreading throughout the compound. There were panicked shouts. Hunt doused some water over his sleeve and tore it off and gave it to Lambert.

"Cover your face from the smoke," Hunt said and coughed violently. He grimaced against the taste of burning diesel and burning flesh.

Hunt heard the rattle of a metal canister and the tell tale hiss and flash of explosions. The quick reaction force was clearing the compound with flash-bangs. Hunt heard them shouting for the two of them.

"Hunt! Lambert! Friendlies! Make yourselves known!"

In unison, the two soldiers yelled, "Over here! End of passage!"

Hunt saw one of the camouflaged figures wearing night vision twist and shine their torches down the smoky-haze and gloom of the corridor. The guys went to stand. A soldier came out of the darkness and said, "Let me see your hands!"

They didn't argue. They put their hands up.

"All right," the American soldier said. "Come on." He grabbed Lambert under the arm and Hunt said, "I'm okay. I'll follow you out."

The guy nodded and took Lambert under his armpit. He shouted to the others, "Over here! We got 'em. Move out!"

"Move out," came the calls as the message echoed from man to man and they passed it down the line. Every man's a link man. Hunt followed them down the passageway and stepped over bodies as he guarded the rear. The smoke grew thicker as they went down the passage towards the interrogation room and so did the pile of bodies.

"Hell of a party," the American said. "Thanks for inviting us."

"Our pleasure," Lambert said and managed a single laugh. "Thanks for joining."

"Yeah, we've saved you some cake!" Hunt said from the back.

They stepped out of the compound. The noise was intense. The room was ablaze. Hunt could hear Apache gunships hovering out of sight providing overwatch. There was still the crack of gunfire and explosions outside the compound walls.

"They're hella dug in," the American yelled to Hunt.

"Yeah, I know." There was an explosion close by and Hunt flinched again. "Goddamn it!" he said.

It was getting very dark. Before they exited the gate of the compound, Hunt grabbed the soldier and twisted him towards him, "Hey!" he shouted trying to speak over the noise and his own ringing ears. "We need to warn Mazar HQ. The enemy is headed to the city!"

"Yeah," the American said. "We got your ICOM message. The Rangers have it covered. C-130s have been strafing the columns and they seem to have disappeared into the local population. Guess they're gonna wait and see ..."

"Having second thoughts," Hunt said.

"How'd you find us," Lambert asked.

"Tracking beacon. Good thinking," the American answered. "Let's go, we need to get to those choppers now!"

"Give me a magazine," Hunt said to him and the yank slapped one in his palm and said, "Let's go."

"FRIENDLIES!" HUNT YELLED AS THEY EXITED THE compound gate. They spilled into the market street. There were cracks of automatic gunfire to the north.

"Sounds like they found some guys who still wanna fight," the American said, then yelled, "Move out!"

The soldiers in the street performed pairs fire and manoeuvre drills and fell back down the streets. There were lots of shouts and confusion from the enemy. The light came from the moon and stars. Hunt could hear the roar of the helicopters in the near distance. The American put his hand to his ear and listened to the radio message.

"Right! We have to move! Move, move, move! Choppers are leaving!"

Everyone sparked up. Hunt nearly felt a sense of relief, they were so close. He turned back and saw the farmer's tractor on fire next to the wall of the compound. A soldier ran past him and tapped him on the shoulder and yelled, "Last man!"

Hunt turned and followed and they all ran in a block out of the village. He vowed to himself that the farmer would get compensation. A medal. A reward. Hearts and minds. Hunt looked ahead into the fields. He saw some of the soldiers jumping over the *wadi* off to his left. His heart sank and he ran forward. "Wait! No!" he yelled. Another one jumped over.

A few of the guys turned to look at him waving his arms. His voice didn't carry far enough with the drone of the rotors. They were clearing the *wadi* at the exact spot Hunt had watched the two figures placing the pressure-pad controlled IED. Maybe they'll make it. Maybe they won't step on it. Maybe they'll make it. Last man.

Boom!

Everyone hit the deck. The air was filled with raining dust and sand and stones. The guys in front of Hunt turned and laid down suppressing fire on the village. Rounds hissed over his head and the machine guns hammered away. Tracer lit up the night. He put his face in the dirt and crawled out of the way. He crawled into the *wadi* to his left. He was disoriented and in shock. He looked back to the village and saw muzzle flashes from roof tops and murder holes. Explosions attract fire. The QRF guys were falling back towards the choppers.

Hunt saw flashes from the village. He aimed and fired a burst. Nothing happened. Stoppage.

"Stoppage!" he doubted they could hear him. He got down lower into the *wadi* and heard something faintly above the gunfire. It was a scared voice.

"Stop! Help. Help me," it shouted.

He frantically looked around and only saw the empty soil and wet mud reflecting the light of the moon in a murky gutter. He couldn't make anything out, only where the trickle of water stopped and started. He listened for the direction of the shouts over the rotors and gunfire. The transport helicopter engines turned faster. They were getting ready to go. Hunt was raging. Someone was still out here! Then he thought he saw something, the outline of a body, or part of a body.

"Help!" Hunt heard again.

"Friendly, friendly!" Hunt yelled. "Can you hear me?"

He moved forward until he reached where he had seen the mass. He lunged forward and felt along under the water. His hand touched something solid and he gripped it and strained to lift it out of the sludge and wetness.

Hunt was holding onto a chest rig and pulled a head up from under the water. It coughed and spat up muddy water. Hunt flopped him down on the bank. He made a quick assessment. This was the soldier hit in the bomb blast, he'd been thrown twenty feet, and he was badly injured. He was missing both legs and an arm.

"What's your name? You still with me?" he said as he checked the wounds.

"I'm here," the guy said.

"I'm going to get you out of here."

Hunt needed to get the soldier to the choppers. It was urgent, triple amputee missing both legs and at least one arm was going to need surgery within one hour. The golden hour. The blast wounds sometimes cauterise, but sometimes they don't. No time to put tourniquets on though. Hunt pulled out a morphine syrette from around the squaddies neck and jabbed it into him. Hunt didn't have his anymore, and even if he did, you give the injured guy his own medicine. Hunt might still need his.

"Are you okay," Hunt said. No response. Hunt slapped his cheek and he groaned.

Aimed shots *snapped* in the air above them. Then there was a *hiss*. Bullets slammed into the mud around them. Spotted.

"We need to move, now!"

Hunt heard the helicopters ready to leave. He climbed out of the ditch with the soldier on his shoulder and sprinted. He ran hard. His chest heaved and he sucked in air. Lactic acid built up in his leg muscles. After a hundred yards he slowed and stumbled, but now he was close. So very close. Stirling ran head down, face against the gusting sand as the light from the choppers lit him and the swirling dust in front of him.

A crewman ran out to meet them. His mouth opened and closed. He was shouting something, waving his arms, but Hunt couldn't hear him over the wind and rotors and his own breathing.

He sprinted hard. His stomach muscles squeezed and released as the body bounced on his shoulders. As he bounced up, Hunt felt like he was hit in the back by a sledgehammer. The punch from the sniper's rifle knocked him forward. He couldn't outrun the momentum, he put his arm out to break the fall and tucked his chin, like a boxer stepping into a punch.

He went down head-first with the soldier's weight on his shoulders. His face hit the dry earth and his world went black.

EPILOGUE

Hunt came round in an intensive care ward. The first sensation he felt was the rough texture of the low count cotton bed linen under his finger tips. And then the smell of iodine and bleach. There was something else. A floral fragrance. A woman's perfume. His fist closed around the bedsheet. He lifted his other hand and felt the plastic tubes on his face that were putting pressure under his nostrils. A crisp white nurse's uniform leaned over his bed and whispered, "Wake up, sailor. We don't want you to die."

She murmured something else, but there was a bell ringing next to his ear and he couldn't make it out clearly. He reached out to pull her closer and his hands clutched at empty air. It was the first thing he remembered after getting knocked unconscious during the exfiltration battle.

Like a bolt latching, he opened his eyes and looked at the nurse standing there. She smiled at him.

"Where am I?" Hunt asked.

"You're back home now. Try not to move, darling. You're in Queen Elizabeth Hospital. You were shot," she said and straightened the bedsheet where he'd creased it.

"Oh," he murmured.

"You were shot trying to save another soldier, do you remember? You have a severe concussion and you've been in an induced coma for some time."

He touched the side of his face. His head was wrapped and eye covered over with bandages. He tried to remember.

"Don't worry," she said as she straightened his sheet and puffed the sides of his pillow. He looked at her with one eye. She had red hair pulled tight under a hat and freckles. He felt her warm breath on his cheek as she looked down at him.

"You're pretty," he said and tried to smile but it turned into a wince. He could always blame the morphine.

"Long voyage was it sailor," she said with a smile and then stepped back. "It seems I have competition for your affections though," and gestured to the flowers on his bedside table. Hunt strained his neck to look and he let out a twinged sigh at the pain.

"Seven white roses," she said and rolled her eyes. "I bet you'll tell me you're married next."

"Who're they from?" Hunt mumbled through his aching jaw. She walked over to the bedside table and snatched up the envelope and the card.

"To Stirling, hell of a job. Pity about missing out on al-Z. See you soon, G.S."

Hunt lay back down. He didn't know who that was. He closed his eyes. He could smell her perfume now she stood close to the bed again. He opened one eye and admired the view. She placed the card back in the bouquet.

"You have some letters too," the nurse said and picked the pile up and gave them to him. "From your grandmother." She pointed to the return address. He took them but didn't look at them. He just lay back with his head resting against the pillows and held the letters in his hand.

"What happened to him?" he asked the nurse and winced again.

"Who?"

"The soldier you mentioned."

"You saved his life. Do you remember what happened?" she asked.

"I remember getting hit—where'd they get me?"

"Well, you were quite lucky, your body armour took most of the rounds. But your pelvis is cracked, that's why you're so sore. Not to worry, we will look after you."

Hunt spent the next few months recovering from the bullet wounds and concussion, and later, he was moved to a Defence Rehabilitation Centre and given a sparse single quarter with a single bed covered in a bright blue duvet cover.

The room had rough grey industrial carpet with laminate furniture, a desk, wardrobe and wash basin in the room. He sat on the edge of the bed and read a letter from his grandmother. Tough coil springs from the old mattress pressed into his wounds.

He read the letter from his last surviving family. While he did, there was a knock, and the door swung open. Hunt looked up and moved to stand, pushing himself up from the bed.

"Hello, Colonel," Hunt said.

"Sit, please," Colonel Rob said. He was a stocky man, shorter than Hunt, with pale freckled skin. He wore the sand coloured beret. He had been ginger once, but the hair on his temples was thinning and grey. He had a thick neck and pale blue eyes that stared at you like he was trying to make out a shape in the dark.

"That was a hell of a thing you did out there, Hunt."

"Thank you, Colonel."

"I wanted to drop by and see you, see how you were doing."

"I am going well, Colonel, stronger every day."

"Good man."

The Colonel pulled the desk chair out and sat down. Hunt sat back on the bed.

"Have you thought about what you will do, Hunt?"

"Sir?"

There was a pause.

"After your rehab. Did you have a job in mind?"

"Back to the Regiment?" Hunt said. It was hopeful.

The Colonel shook his head. Hunt looked down quickly and back up at the Colonel. He opened his mouth to speak, but closed it again. The Colonel leaned forward.

"If it was up to me, you would stay in the Regiment," he said softly. Hunt's eyes darted over the Colonel's face. "Come and see me when you are mobile, I will make sure you get something interesting at Forces Command."

"An office job?"

"You've had your time in the field, Captain Hunt. You were incredibly effective and you're a hell of an operator. One of the best. But it's time to be effective somewhere else now."

"Thank you, sir. But, you know that isn't me."

"You look frustrated, Hunt."

He felt frustrated. The only thing keeping him sane and enduring the inane was the thought of getting back on the front line. Al-Zawahiri was still out there. They sat and looked at one another for a moment.

"Let me try again," the Colonel said. "In my experience there are only a few reasons people join up. One, they need the money and have no prospects. Two, for some like myself, it's expected. A family trade. Third, the glory hunters who fight for Queen and country. Which one are you? What's driving you, Hunt?"

Hunt thought for a moment. There was no way he would go into detail about Kelly with this man, so he stuck to his practiced routine.

"My father was a Selous Scout and fought in the Bush War against the communists."

"Rhodesia," the Colonel said, stone faced.

"Yes."

"So, a family trade. What does he think about all of this?"

"I don't know, Colonel. My parents were killed before I was sent away to England."

They sat in silence again. Hunt wondered if this man knew that he'd watched his father bleed to death when he was a boy. Or that they had found his mother's mutilated body, charred, and disfigured in a nearby dump.

"I only have one clear memory of my father, aside from the night he died. We would go out shooting with the rifle he gave me. He would say, 'know—really *know*—what you are going to do before you do it'. And, ever since, I've tried to. And not only when it comes to shooting. I joined the Marines to learn how to do it."

"Do what, Captain?"

"Whatever was required, sir. Whatever is needed to get the job done. Just to know that I won't allow what happened to my parents to happen to anyone that I care about. Does that answer your question?"

The Colonel nodded slowly and took a more fatherly tone. "Let me be clear, for all you have done – and we owe you a lot – you are your own worst enemy. I've never known anyone who acts with so little regard for their own self-interest. And I think you are still trying to live up to the expectations of the idea of a man you will never see again," the Colonel paused. "I know you won't stop until it's killed you. But bury your demons, son. Bury them deep. Move on."

"I can't do that, Colonel. I made them a promise."

"Well then," the Colonel looked solemn, "Follow your father's advice, and know what you are going to do."

The Colonel put his hand out, Hunt gripped it.

"Oh, I have something for you. They've given you this." The Colonel pulled out a blue felt covered box. Hunt clicked it open and read the note. *In recognition of an act or acts of conspicuous gallantry during active operations against the enemy.* He closed the box and set it down.

"This must be what old dogs feel like," Hunt said and half-smiled, "On a one-way trip to the vet."

The Colonel watched him and he looked wounded.

"I've always known you as a stoic, Hunt. Don't look so pained." He moved to the door then stopped and turned back. "You look well, Stirling. Fighting fit. Better than I expected, considering ... If it were only up to me," he opened his arms apologetically. Hunt nodded and felt like he had been hit in the gut. The blood ran from his face.

"Good luck."

And that was it. Thanks for your service, goodbye. Hunt sat with his head in his hands. His career was over. He was lost in his own thoughts. He didn't know how long he sat there, and didn't hear the door swing open again.

"Um, Mr Hunt?"

Hunt looked up. A man who looked like Churchill's grandson stood in his room. The first thing Hunt noticed was the shine of his shoes. The second, how his lower jaw jutted forward and loose double chin rolled over his starched collar under a double breasted pinstripe suit.

Hunt stood up. "Who are you?"

"I am a friend, Mr Hunt, a friend."

"Well, whatever you are selling, I'm not buying. I have life insurance, thanks."

"Ah, well, where you're going you might just need a little more. What do you say? Hear me out and I will be out of your hair, two shakes of a lamb's tail."

Hunt sat down, "Okay, I'm all ears."

"Do you mind if I sit?"

Hunt gestured to the chair and the man sat down and crossed his legs. He looked at Hunt, breathing through his mouth, until Hunt cleared his throat and looked away uncomfortably.

"Have you ever wondered why your family were murdered?"

Hunt narrowed his eyes. Who the hell does he think he is, he thought and wondered about this bulldog of a man sitting in front of him.

"They were murdered during a farm invasion in Rhodesia. A heinous crime. But not an uncommon one, unfortunately."

"We say Zimbabwe now, don't we?"

"Do we?" Hunt replied.

"Tell me, Mr Hunt. Suppose you wanted to murder someone, do you think a good way would be to make it look like something more ordinary, more mundane?" "Mundane?" Hunt repeated. He was angry. "I've had about enough of this," and moved to get up.

"It wasn't a farm invasion, Mr Hunt. It was an assassination. Wouldn't you like to know who is responsible for killing your parents?" Hunt calmed, and sat back down.

"I'm listening," he said. "Ah, buying what I am selling now, are we, Mr Hunt?"

"Maybe. Why are you telling me this?"

"How would you like the opportunity to take revenge, hmm?"

He slid a black-and-white photograph across the desk and

Hunt looked at it. "Do you recognise this man? You may have seen him before. The night your father died?"

Hunt shook his head. He couldn't be sure. He had seen someone that night. A man in a balaclava. But he only remembered the eyes. Pale, opaline green eyes. That man had pulled a bloody panga from his father's back.

"Maybe, maybe not."

"That is a picture of Aslan Kabazanov from the early nineties. Aka, the Scorpion. Ex-Colonel in the KGB, and current Chechen warlord involved in every vice from arms dealing to sex trafficking. And, the man responsible for killing your parents."

Hunt looked at the picture again, more closely. He shook his head, and looked up. "Who the hell are you?"

"So sorry, how rude. Please allow me to introduce myself. I am Gerald D. Soames, Secret Intelligence Service, but please, call me Gerry."

What the hell was MI6 doing here? Soames perched himself on the edge of the chair, still breathing through his mouth. "Do you have some kind of identification?" Hunt asked.

"No, I don't," Soames said with a half-grin, jaw jutting forward.

"So how do I–"

Soames cut him off. "So, what'll it be, Captain, a cushy desk job at headquarters? Or, do you want to come and work for me and bring down one of the worst organised crime threats to Her Majesty's Government, and more importantly, avenge your parents?"

"You want me to be a spy?"

"If that is what you want to call it, we say covert operative. But, what we call it doesn't matter. What we really want is you, and for you to be yourself; with an ulterior motive. You will need to become very good at pretending to be someone else, while being yourself–do you understand?"

"No cover story?"

"Cover? You will be hiding in plain sight, my boy. You already have the best cover for this mission. We will send you in as a mercenary. Wounded ex-war hero, honourably discharged, becomes a gun runner in west Africa and falls in with the wrong crowd. What's not to love?"

"Smuggling guns in Africa?"

"Initially, yes. We need you to rock the boat. Step on some toes. And, we can arrange a supplier as a starting point." Hunt nodded along, deep in thought. Planning. Soames could see it on his face. "But, understand this is a black op, Hunt. It is all real, not make believe. No one is 'in on it'. It's real and if you do this willingly, you are alone. Off the books. Plausible deniability. We aren't coming in with the cavalry to get you if you get into trouble. You can check in once a week with me or not at all. Officially you do not work for MI6, and we will not help you. Confirm to me that you understand."

"I understand," he said. "And training?"

"Training? Why, what more training do you want, Hunt? Her Majesty's Government has already invested enough in you. Weapons, covert ops and self-defence expert, you were the naval boxing champion, if I am not mistaken? You speak three languages. And, you were born in Africa. Have I missed anything?"

Hunt shook his head. Soames pinched his flabby neck between forefinger and thumb and pulled at the skin.

"No, my boy," he said thoughtfully. "Usually, recruitment like this takes time. And, if you choose to accept this mission, when you are healed, you are heading to Angola. In the meantime, we can help you prepare, and use your rehabilitation wisely. You will study, plan and prepare. Once in-country, we can give you some help to get started, make some introductions, point out the way, but once you are there, there you are. On your own. Understand?"

Hunt sat very still with the tinnitus ringing in his ear, and looked through Soames, as his mind moved through the consequences step-by-step, like the moves on a chess board.

"Is there a file?"

"Just the photograph for now," Soames said. But it was grainy and taken from far away. "There, in the middle," he said and waved his finger. "Beret and sunglasses, from the Chechen war." Hunt studied the picture again and searched the recess of his mind. He had no clear image of this man. He didn't remember him. But he knew he hated him.

"Will he know who I am?"

"Our intelligence says not," Soames said. "So, what'll it be, yes or no?"

Hunt felt he was pushing for an answer. His mind strayed to the day he buried his parents. It was a wet day. He'd stood in a dark suit. The misty rain had seeped through, and stuck the fabric to his skin. He'd placed a wreath, and leaned it against the headstones. There was so much to say, and also nothing. And the anger never left. He'd just stood there with his head bowed, saying nothing, looking at the slabs of stone, until long after the other mourners had gone inside for sweet tea and triangular sandwiches. He'd sworn then that he would find out who killed them, and do something about it. This was his chance. He knew his destiny lay on the continent of his birth; and of his parents' death. What place isn't home, if it isn't where your dead are buried? "Does this operation have a name?" Hunt asked. "Eostrix. An owl that eats scorpions, apparently. The green slime are swots like that," Soames replied.

"Okay, Mr Soames. Yes, I'll do it."

Soames nodded. "Good decision."

"Can I just ask ..." Hunt said.

"Anything."

"What about al-Zawahiri? What I mean is, is he still alive?"

"Yes, he's alive. And don't worry, my boy. We'll get him next time. Or, to be more precise, you will ..."

BLOOD FEUD

AN EXCERPT

A STIRLING HUNT THRILLER

STEWART CLYDE

BLOOD FEUD

If you like **Frederick Forsyth** you'll love **Stewart Clyde**

HIS CODE IS LOYALTY. HIS MISSION IS REVENGE.

Published by Hunt Press in 2020.

Copyright © Stewart Clyde 2020.

The moral right of Stewart Clyde to be identified as the Author of the Work has been asserted by him, in accordance with the Copyrights, Designs and Patents Act 1988.

All rights reserved. No part of this publication may be reproduced, stored in a retrieval system, or transmitted in any form or by any means without prior permission in writing from the publisher.

First published in 2020 by Hunt Press.

First published in Great Britain.

All characters are fictitious and any resemblance to real persons, living or dead, is purely coincidental.

CONTENTS

Read the next instalment now	183
Chapter 1	185
Chapter 2	204
Chapter 3	212

READ THE NEXT INSTALMENT NOW

Press here to read: Blood Feud - A Gripping Assassination Thriller (A Stirling Hunt Mission, Book 2)

CHAPTER ONE

Matadi, Angola

THE PLASTIC EXPLOSIVE lay next to him on the front seat, neatly bundled in pink happy birthday wrapping paper. Stirling rested his bush hat on top of it, and drew up to a line of cars and buses waiting at the border to cross into the Congo. He gave the package no thought. It was perfectly obvious, which made it perfectly safe. The short-bonnet truck vibrated and rattled and his hands shook as he lit a cigarette. He wound down the window and felt the mid-morning heat settle around the truck.

A drop of sweat ran to the tip of his nose. It had been hot since sunrise and was getting hotter. The exchange was scheduled for before dawn, but he'd gotten a puncture and had spent hours by the side of a dark road fighting to get the wheel off.

He tapped the ash out of the window and saw a group of

children running towards him with hands outstretched and wide smiles.

"Sweets, sweets!" they chorused.

Stirling smiled and spoke in Swahili to them.

"I have sweets for you, if you can get me across the border faster."

They looked at one another and then the tallest boy stepped forward in a torn brown shirt and red shorts.

"Me, I know who can help you," he said.

"Okay. Go and get them then."

"No, first sweets!"

Stirling leaned down, pulled out some lollies from a packet and dished them out to happy faces. The kids pushed forward and swarmed around, yelling with hands outstretched to grab the sweets as they fell. The tallest boy stuck a sucker in his mouth and ran barefoot away from the truck.

The kids played and danced next to the front tyre while Stirling took a long drag on his cigarette and shifted his weight on the sticky brown leather seat. He looked down the line of cars to the Angolan customs in their blue uniforms. They weren't inspecting much of anything. Stirling had chosen this border crossing because it was hot and crowded at this time of day, and he thought the guards would be lethargic. Angolan customs were nonchalant, and even more relaxed if they were bribed. It didn't normally take much.

He sat alone in the truck and the diesel engine chuntered hypnotically. It was sweltering. Stirling felt the rivulets of sweat slide down his back, and it reminded him of being in the back of a chopper over the mountains of Afghanistan. He closed his eyes and shook his head when the flashback came to snap himself out of it and stay in the present, but it was no use.

In his head, he was back there, and felt vertigo as the helicopter careened, flying fast and low, eighty feet off the ground. It dipped and shook, and Stirling stared dead ahead as the noise and vibrations rattled up his spine. It was hot, and in body armour, like sitting under a blanket in the sun. The inside was spartan. Cracked cyalume sticks gave the hull a radiation green glow and the deck was covered in grease and sand. The taste of aviation fuel sat at the back of his throat.

The men around him were wedged together on the floor. Their bodies sagged as they relaxed their muscles against the weight of the gear. No one spoke. Even if they had, the *zshh-zshh-zshh* of the rotor-blades drowned out any sound.

He snapped himself back with a big breath in, and realised his heart was pounding. Stirling concentrated on his breathing and loosened his grip on the steering wheel, and colour flowed back to his white knuckles. He could feel the spring under the seat pressing into his backside and his old wounds ached. He wriggled to find some relief. He'd spent months in pain on his back in a hospital bed, unable to move, uncomfortable and sore.

AND THERE HE WAS ONCE AGAIN, ON HIS BACK IN THE intensive care ward, while a crisp white nurses' uniform leaned over his bed and whispered, "Wake up, sailor, we don't want you to die."

She murmured something else, but there was a dinner bell ringing next to his ear and he couldn't make it out clearly. He reached out to pull her closer and his hands clutched at empty air.

It was the first thing he remembered after getting knocked unconscious during the battle. Like a bolt latching, he opened his eyes and looked at the nurse standing there. She smiled at him.

"Where am I?"

"You're back home now. Try not to move, darling. You're in Queen Elizabeth Hospital. You were shot," she said and straightened the bedsheet.

"Oh."

"You were shot trying to save another soldier, do you remember? You have a severe concussion and you've been in an induced coma for some time."

He touched the side of his face. His head was wrapped and eye covered over with bandages. He tried to remember. The ringing in his ears sounded like the helicopters in-bound. He caught snippets, moment of events, like a dream. He remembered the explosion, and the injured trooper on his shoulder. He remembered running, and how, after a thousand yards he'd slowed and stumbled. The casevac helicopter kicking up dust, like it was the surface of the moon, and running head down, his face against the gusting sand.

A crewman had run out to meet them. He'd shouted, but Stirling couldn't hear him over the wind and rotors and his own breathing. He'd sprinted hard, and his stomach squeezed and released as the soldier bounced up and down. And, he remembered the feeling of getting hit in the back with a sledgehammer. The punch from the bullets knocking him forward, and how he'd put his arm out and tucked in his chin to break the fall, like a boxer stepping into a punch, his face hit the dry riverbed with the weight of the trooper on his neck.

"What happened to him?" he asked the nurse, and winced at the pain.

"You saved his life. He's in a room down the corridor."

"Do you remember what happened?" she asked.

"I remember getting hit – where'd they get me?"

"Well, you were quite lucky, your body armour took most

of the rounds. But your pelvis is cracked, that's why you're so sore. Not to worry, we will look after you."

He spent the next few months recovering from the bullet wounds and later, he was moved to a Defence Rehabilitation Centre and given a sparse single quarter with a single bed covered in a bright blue duvet. The room had rough grey industrial carpet with laminate furniture, a desk, wardrobe and wash basin in the room. He sat on the edge of the bed and read a letter from his grandmother, while tough coil springs from the old mattress pressed into his wounds. He read:

Dear Stirling,

My move is: Nf3

We missed you at Gramps's funeral. I am so glad you are recovering well ...

There was a chess board on the desk and he moved the Knight. He'd been playing, via correspondence, with his grandmother since the hospital. She thought it would help with his recovery and critical faculty, and she was right. There was a knock and the door swung open. Stirling looked up from the board and moved to stand, pushing himself up from the bed.

"Hello, Colonel," Stirling said.

"Sit, please," Colonel Rob said. He was a stocky man, shorter than Stirling, with pale freckled skin. He wore the sand coloured beret. He had been ginger once, but the hair on his temples was thinning and grey. He had a thick neck and pale blue eyes that stared at you like he was trying to make out a shape in the dark.

"That was a hell of a thing you did out there, Hunt."

"Thank you, Colonel."

"I wanted to drop by and see you, see how you were doing."

"I am going well, Colonel, stronger every day."

"Good man."

The Colonel pulled the desk chair out and sat down. Stirling sat back on the bed.

"Have you thought about what you will do, Hunt?"

"Sir?"

There was a pause.

"After your rehab. Did you have a job in mind?"

"Back to the Regiment?" Stirling offered hopefully.

The Colonel shook his head. Stirling looked down quickly and back up at the Colonel. He opened his mouth to speak, but closed it again. The Colonel leaned forward.

"If it was up to me, you would stay in the Regiment," he said softly.

Stirling's eyes darted over the Colonel's face.

"Come and see me when you are mobile, I will make sure you get something interesting at Forces Command."

"An office job?"

"You've had your time in the field, Captain Hunt. You were incredibly effective and you're a hell of an operator. One of the best. But it's time to be effective somewhere else now."

"Thank you, sir. But, you know that isn't me."

"You look frustrated, Hunt."

He felt frustrated. The only thing keeping him sane and enduring the inane was the thought of getting back on the front line. They sat and looked at one another for a moment.

"Let me try again," the Colonel said. "In my experience there are only a few reasons people join up. One, they need the money and have no prospects. Two, for some like myself, it's expected. A family trade. Third, the glory hunters who fight for Queen and country. Which one are you? What's driving you Hunt?"

Stirling thought a moment.

"My father was a Selous Scout and fought in the Bush War against the communists."

"Rhodesia," the Colonel said, stone faced.

"Yes."

"So, a family trade. What does he think about all of this?"

"I don't know, Colonel. My parents were killed before I was sent away, to England."

They sat in silence again. Stirling wondered if this man knew that he'd watched his father bleed to death when he was a boy. Or that they had found his mother's mutilated body, charred and disfigured in a nearby dump.

"I only have one clear memory of my father, aside from the night he died. We would go out shooting with the rifle he gave me. He would say, 'know – *really know* – what you are going to do before you do it'. And, ever since, I have tried to. And not only when it comes to shooting. I joined the Marines to learn how to do it."

"Do what, Captain?"

"Whatever was required, sir. Whatever is needed to get the job done. Just to know that I won't allow what happened to my parents to happen to anyone that I care about. Does that answer your question?"

The Colonel nodded slowly and took a more fatherly tone.

"Let me be clear, for all you have done – and we owe you a lot – you are your own worst enemy. I've never known anyone who acts with so little regard for their own self-interest. And I think you are still trying to live up to the expectations of the idea of a man you will never see again," the Colonel paused. "I know you won't stop until it's killed you. But bury your demons, son. Bury them deep. Move on."

"I can't do that, Colonel. I made them a promise."

"Well then," the Colonel looked solemn, "follow your father's advice, and know what you are going to do."

The Colonel put his hand out, Stirling gripped it.

"Oh, I have something for you. They've given you this."

The Colonel pulled out a blue felt covered box. Stirling clicked it open and read the note. *In recognition of an act or acts of conspicuous gallantry during active operations against the enemy.* He closed the box and set it down.

"This must be what old dogs feel like," Stirling said and half-smiled, "on a one-way trip to the vet."

The Colonel watched him and he looked wounded.

"I've always known you as a stoic, Hunt. Don't look so pained."

He moved to the door then stopped and turned back.

"You look well, Stirling. Fighting fit. Better than I expected considering ... If it were only up to me," he opened his arms apologetically. Stirling nodded and felt like he had been hit in the gut; the blood ran from his face.

"Good luck."

And that was it. Thanks for your service, goodbye.

Stirling sat with his head in his hands. His career was over. He was lost in his own thoughts. He didn't know how long he sat there, and didn't hear the door swing open again.

"Um, Mr Hunt?"

Stirling looked up. A man who looked like Churchill's grandson stood in his room. The first thing Stirling noticed was the shine of his shoes. The second, how his lower jaw jutted forward and loose double chin rolled over his starched collar under a double breasted pinstriped suit.

Stirling stood up. "Who are you?"

"I am a friend, Mr Hunt, a friend."

"Well, whatever you are selling, I'm not buying. I have life insurance, thanks."

"Ah, well, where you're going you might just need a little more. What do you say? Hear me out and I will be out of your hair, two shakes of a lamb's tail."

Stirling sat down, "Okay, I'm all ears."

"Do you mind if I sit?"

Stirling gestured to the chair and the man sat down and crossed his legs. He looked at Stirling, breathing through his mouth, until Stirling cleared his throat and looked away uncomfortably.

"Have you ever wondered why your family were murdered?"

Stirling narrowed his eyes. *Who the hell does he think he is*, he thought and wondered about this bulldog of a man sitting in front of him.

"They were murdered during a farm invasion in Rhodesia. A heinous crime. But not an uncommon one, unfortunately."

"We say Zimbabwe now, don't we?"

"Do we?" Stirling replied.

"Tell me, Mr Hunt. Suppose you wanted to murder someone, do you think a good way would be to make it look like something more ordinary, more mundane?"

"Mundane?" Stirling repeated. He was angry. "I've had about enough of this," and moved to get up.

"It wasn't a farm invasion, Mr Hunt. It was an assassination. Wouldn't you like to know who is responsible for killing your parents?"

Stirling calmed, and sat back down.

"I'm listening," he said.

"Ah, buying what I am selling now, are we, Mr Hunt?

"Maybe. Why are you telling me this?"

"How would you like the opportunity to take revenge, hmm?" He slid a black-and-white photograph across the desk and Stirling looked at it. "Do you recognise this man? You may have seen him before. The night your father died?"

Stirling shook his head. He couldn't be sure. He had seen someone that night. A man in a balaclava. But he only remembered the eyes. Pale, opaline green eyes. That man had pulled a bloody *panga* from his father's back.

"Maybe, maybe not."

"That is a picture of Aslan Kabazanov from the early nineties. Aka, the Scorpion. Ex-Colonel in the KGB, and current Chechen warlord involved in every vice from arms dealing to sex trafficking. And, the man responsible for killing your parents."

Stirling looked at the picture again, more closely. He shook his head, and looked up.

"Who the hell are you?"

"So sorry, how rude. Please allow me to introduce myself. I am Gerald D. Soames, Secret Intelligence Service, but please, call me Gerry."

What the hell is MI6 doing here?

Soames perched himself on the edge of the chair, still breathing through his mouth.

"Do you have some kind of identification?" Stirling asked.

"No, I don't," Soames said with a half-grin, jaw jutting forward.

"So how do I – "

Soames cut him off.

"So, what'll it be, Captain, a cushy desk job at headquarters? Or, do you want to come and work for me and bring down one of worst organised crime threats to Her Majesty's Government, and more importantly, avenge your parents?"

"You want me to be a spy?"

"If that is what you want to call it, we say covert operative. But, what we call it doesn't matter. What we really want is you, and for you to be yourself; with an ulterior motive. You will need to become very good at pretending to be someone else, while being yourself – do you understand?"

"No cover story?"

"Cover? You will be hiding in plain sight, my boy. You already have the best cover for this mission. We will send you in as a mercenary. Wounded ex-war hero, honourably discharged, becomes a gun runner in west Africa and falls in with the wrong crowd. What's not to love?"

"Smuggling guns in Africa?"

"Initially, yes. We need you to rock the boat. Step on some toes. And, we can arrange a supplier as a starting point."

Stirling nodded along, deep in thought. Planning. Soames could see it on his face.

"But, understand this is a black op, Hunt. It is all real, not make believe. No one is 'in on it'. It's real and if you do this willingly, you are alone. Off the books. Plausible deniability. We aren't coming in with the cavalry to get you if you get into trouble. You can check in once a week with me or not at all. Officially you do not work for MI6, and we will not help you. Confirm to me that you understand."

"I understand," he said. "And training?"

"Training? Why, what more training do you want, Hunt? Her Majesty's Government has already invested enough in you. Weapons, covert ops and self-defence expert, you were the naval boxing champion, if I am not mistaken? You speak three languages. And, you were born in Africa. Have I missed anything?"

Stirling shook his head. Soames pinched his flabby neck between forefinger and thumb and pulled at the skin.

"No, my boy," he said thoughtfully. "Usually, recruitment like this takes time. And, if you choose to accept this mission, when you are healed, you are heading to Angola. In the meantime, we can help you prepare, and use your rehabilitation wisely. You will study, plan and prepare. Once in-country, we can give you some help to get started, make some introductions, point out the way, but once you are there, there you are. On your own. Understand?"

Stirling sat very still with the tinnitus ringing in his ear, and looked through Soames, as his mind moved through the consequences step-by-step, like the moves on a chess board.

"Is there a file?"

"Just the photograph for now," Soames said.

But it was grainy and taken from far away.

"There, in the middle," he said and waved his finger. "Beret and sunglasses, from the Chechen war."

Stirling studied the picture again and searched the recess of his mind. He had no clear image of this man. He didn't remember him. But he knew he hated him.

"Will he know who I am?"

"Our intelligence says not," Soames said. "So, what'll it be, yes or no?"

Stirling felt he was pushing for an answer.

His mind strayed to the day he buried his parents. It was a wet day. He'd stood in a dark suit. The misty rain had seeped through, and stuck the fabric to his skin. He'd placed a wreath, and leaned it against the headstones. There was so much to say, and also nothing. And the anger never left.

He'd just stood there with his head bowed, saying nothing, looking at the slabs of stone, until long after the other mourners had gone inside for sweet tea and triangular sandwiches. He'd sworn then that he would find out who killed them, and do something about it.

This was his chance. He knew his destiny lay on the continent of his birth; and of his parents' death.

What place isn't home, if it isn't where your dead are buried?

"Does this operation have a name?" Stirling asked.

"Eostrix. An owl that eats scorpions, apparently. The green slime are swots like that," Soames replied.

"Okay, Mr Soames. Yes, I'll do it."

After Soames left, he made his move, and castled his king. His grandfather had been the chess champion of Rhodesia at one time. And his grandmother had beaten him on occasion, as she's subtly mentioned in a letter, while politely challenging him to a match. They'd played several games over the months. He sat at the desk, rejuvenated, and wrote a to her.

Dearest Granny,
My move is: 0-0
Wonderful news. I hope to see you soon, I'll be back in Africa much sooner than we'd thought ...

The day after his discharge, he gained a berth on a cargo ship headed for the west coast of Africa, his passage negotiated in exchange for providing maritime security on board. After weeks on the lookout for pirates, Stirling arrived in Luanda, the capital of the old Portuguese colony in Angola.

The country had been ravaged by a civil war, but was rich in minerals and unexplored tropical jungle. The price of oil boomed and Luanda had become the Geneva of Africa. And Stirling set out on his mission to put himself between the Government, organised crime and the private security sector. The exact place those looking to profit from misery could be found.

He finished his cigarette and mashed it on the dashboard. The tall boy appeared, put his hands to his mouth, whistled and waved Stirling forward.

"Good boy," he said and the old diesel engine pulled him past the row of parked cars and buses. Each was full of people, some with luggage on the roof, some with cages of chickens or livestock. Everyone stared at the truck and some spat. He pulled up opposite the sentry post with a boom gate across the dirt road and the brakes whined as he came to a stop. The border guard stepped out from his hut and flopped his beret on top of his fat round head. Stirling leaned out window and looked down.

"Russian, or English?" the guard asked.

"English please, chief."

The border guard looked surprised.

"Documents."

Stirling handed him his passport and a bit of paper and the inspector flicked through it.

"Cigarettes?" he asked, looking at the passport.

"No," Stirling said.

"Alcohol?"

"No."

"What then?" the inspector asked.

"Medical supplies for the Christian Mission in DRC."

"Alone?"

"Yes."

"Where is it?" the inspector asked.

"Kinshasa. That paper tells you," Stirling said. It was a typed letter on official looking headed paper. Stirling was sure the border guard couldn't read it.

"Show me," the guard said, moving to the back of the truck. Stirling climbed down and unhinged the tailgate and it dropped with a bang. He climbed onto the flatbed and opened the first wooden box and held the lid open for the inspector.

"See?" Stirling said, "Only bandages and plasters." He didn't mention that the other crates were full of rifles and grenades and covered over with the medical supplies. The guard gave the box a cursory look and took out a handkerchief to dab the beading sweat from his face and neck.

"It is very hot," he said and gestured outside. Stirling watched him. They were doing the customary dance around one another now. Stirling saw a glint in his eye and the corner of his mouth turn up slightly.

"But, we are so very thirsty," the guard said and wrinkled his eyebrows like a puppy.

"Yes, it is very hot," Stirling agreed solemnly. "If it might help our situation here, I have soft drinks in the truck ... maybe a cold Coke for you and your colleague?"

The inspector grinned.

"I suppose we have a deal," Stirling said. "After you," and ushered him off the back of the wagon.

He drove past the guard hut and the inspector took a sip of Coke and beamed his African smile. Stirling waved at them as he crossed into the Congo.

"Thank you very much, gentlemen."

He felt good. The first score in his new life was just down this dusty track, if he could survive the heat.

Northern Angola was sparse and empty. The Congo was like going back in time, and almost unchanged from the time of Dr Livingstone.

Stirling kept one eye on the gravel path as it came bouncing up in front of him, and pulled out a neatly folded map, open to the grid squares he needed. He checked his watch and position and calculated it in his head. Kinshasa was two-hundred and five miles away. On this bumpy, badly graded road he would do an average of thirty miles hour: that meant a seven-hour drive.

He had run out of jingles and snippets of pop songs to hum and checked his watch. He'd only been going for an hour. It felt like at least two. He exhaled in forceful boredom and drummed both hands on the steering wheel and looked out at the thick tunnel of green bush around the truck.

Stirling flicked on the radio and it hissed. He took his eyes off the road to tune it and when he looked up from the orange needle there was a man with an AK-47 rifle standing in the middle of the road. He thought for a second about just driving him over, but the rebel lifted the rifle and pulled the trigger.

"Shit!"

He jammed his foot hard onto the pedal. He felt the rusted brake drums clamp and the wheels locked as the shot *zipped* over the roof. The truck skidded on the gravel and Stirling felt the cargo shift. There was a quiet moment as the dust drifted, and then like vultures around a carcass, rebels were around the truck pointing soviet-era rifles and screeching at him to get down and get out.

He ducked out of sight and stuffed the map and a compass in his cargo trousers. He grabbed a small revolver from the glove box and tucked it into his crotch and broke the key off in the ignition. One of the rebels pulled open the driver's side door and barked at him.

"Get down, climb down now!"

"Okay-okay!" Stirling put his hands above his head and sat up. The rebel was wild-eyed from *khat* and Stirling saw needle scars on his arm. The drug-crazed ambusher stepped back from the door, pointed his rifle and shouted in a heavy west African accent.

"Move you *maggot*, get outta da truck, get down. Now!"

Stirling slid out, making deliberate and slow movements. He didn't want to give them any more reason to kill him than they already had. He was in trouble and the adrenaline kicked in. His breathing was shallow and the fear crept up the base of his skull and stuck in his throat. He stood next to the cab with his hands next to his head. The rebel spat at him and grabbed him by the front of the shirt, Stirling didn't resist. He pulled him and kicked Stirling on the back of his leg. He fell forward onto his hands and knees and felt the heat of the sun on his back and the warmth of the dust under his palms.

A shadow moved over his hands in the dust. He looked up and squinted at another rebel's face. He wore cheap mirrored aviators and had blotches of pink skin in places, like he had been burned, or born disfigured. He was obscured by the glare of the sun. The man pulled a lit cigarette from his mouth and exhaled the smoke through gritted teeth. He held it forward and offered it to Stirling.

"No thanks," Stirling said. "I've just quit."

The rebel shrugged.

"Dis may be your last chance," he said. "So tink careful."

The other ambushers climbed into the truck and threw equipment out of the cab. Stirling flinched as the pink birthday present of plastic explosive hit the ground.

One leaned out from the rear and shouted in Congolese French, "*Nous avons les fusils!*" We have the guns.

The rebel leader stood in front of Stirling and scoffed.

"You see? You are a stupid man." He spoke slowly and with the same accent as the others. "Coming alone into Congo," he shook his head and tutted.

"This cargo is for the big man in Kinshasa," Stirling said trying to sound ominous. The rebel sucked his brown teeth.

"*Il dit qu'ils sont quelqu'un d'important*," he said loudly to the others and they all laughed. He looked at Stirling again.

"I don't think they are worried who it is for. You think I work for myself?" he asked rhetorically and twisted his arm so Stirling could see the "LRA" brand on his shoulder. The scar tissue was raised and blotched. Stirling realised he was getting ripped off by the same people he was supposed to be selling the shipment to.

"You're Lord's Resistance Army? This cargo is for Joseph."

"Cold Killer, *regarde le*," the rebel said to the man behind Stirling. "This is Cold Killer. If you move, he will kill you."

The rebel leader walked past him. Cold Killer looked at Stirling with a depraved grin and dried snot on his lip. His eyes were a watery yellow, a sure sign of malaria. He jabbed Stirling in the temple with his AK-47 and Stirling looked at the ground in submission and clenched his jaw in frustration.

"I am not going to die here," he said under his breath.

"Hey, you, English! Where da explosive?" the rebel leader shouted from behind him. He came up and grabbed Stirling's face.

"I only ask once, English." His lips opened in a sly grin, relishing this part.

"Where da explosive!?" He let go of Stirling's face and slapped him across the jaw. Stirling felt the burn of the strike on his cheek and stared blankly straight into the mirrored lenses.

"I am going to kill you," he said matter-of-factly through gritted teeth.

The rebel laughed and removed his sunglasses. Stirling saw he had a long scar across one eye, it was creamy white and blind.

"No, English." He shook his head, "I am going to kill *you*. Right now." He reached into his pocket and pulled out two clear plastic vials. "You see? I am going to scoop up your blood and get a promotion. Climb the corporate ladder, eh?"

He laughed and looked at Cold Killer and said, "Hey, *wena, tue-le maintenant.*"

Cold Killer cocked his rifle.

"Say your prayers," the leader grinned. Cold Killer pressed the rifle into Stirling's temple.

"Yes, yes. I want to say my prayers. Please," Stirling said.

Cold Killer looked at the rebel leader, unsure.

Stirling lifted his hands in front of his face in prayer and started, "Our Father, who art in heaven ..."

The rebel leader's laugh boomed, Cold Killer shouted in Stirling's ear and jabbed him in the temple. In one action, Stirling brushed the barrel past his head with the back of his hand and reached into his crotch for the revolver. Stirling saw the yellows of the savage eyes widen as he squeezed the trigger. The front of Cold Killer's neck exploded and he dropped his rifle to plug the hole with both hands. The gore seeped through his fingers as he choked on his own blood.

The gunshot echoed around them and off the truck and the trees, and the birds took flight. As the sound died away, Cold Killer dropped and gurgled his last breath into the dirt. Stirling was up quickly. He grabbed the pink wrapped box and a clump of the rebel leader's Afro in the other hand and yanked him yelling to the cover of the thicket on their flank.

"*Déglingue le! Déglingue le!*" Shoot him! he screamed at the others as Stirling dragged him to the cover of the bushes. The rebels yelled back and fired a volley over Stirling's head.

"They don't want to shoot you," Stirling grunted as he pulled the man away. He stopped at the edge of the bush and turned back to face the truck.

"But I do ..." he said into his ear. "Who set me up?"

"*Déglingue le!*" the rebel shouted again to his men. They looked at one another. Stirling put the revolver to his temple. "*Déglingue le!*" he screamed desperately.

Stirling closed one eye and turned his face away and pulled the trigger. The blood splatter hit him on the cheek and neck, and the body fell into the grass.

CHAPTER TWO

The Mediterranean Sea

He took a sip of his Scotch with ice and looked out at the white pebble beaches and green rocky coast line. He stood on the upper deck of his prized possession, his super-yacht Helios, wearing a too tight blue speedo and too loose gold jewellery. He'd taken it from a Russian oligarch by making him an offer he couldn't refuse. The yacht in exchange for not killing his daughter.

He sucked his top lip and tasted the peat and pulsed his forearm, so the scorpion tattoo covering it twisted and moved, as if it was crawling under his skin, and then slammed the crystal tumbler down hard enough that he thought it might break. The girl near him on the sofa jumped and quivered.

"Read it to me. Read it to me, you *bitch*. You don't read English? Or what?" He spoke in a Chechen dialect of Russian.

It was the tonal match of bumping into furniture in the dark. The girl was wearing a bikini and high heels, and she was balled up in the corner of the L-shaped sofa. She watched him through the brown hair that hung in her face and trembled.

"Maybe if I *fuck* you like my teacher fucked me, you'll learn to read."

She yelped. He climbed onto the sofa and leered. He leaned forward, his mouth close to her ear.

"Can you read English?" he rasped.

"Yes," she said quietly.

His voice grew louder and crescendoed, "So, read it and tell me what it says, in Russian!" He snatched the book from her hands and she cowered. He held it with both hands and looked at the cover, a copy of *The International Jew* by Henry Ford.

"This is a great book, by a great American," he said spitting the words. "I must know what it says." He raised the book and hit the girl across the face with it. The blow knocked her head back and he felt his dick harden in his speedo. This was turning him on. He moved to strike her again.

"Sir, a call for you," a voice said urgently behind him. It was his valet, Dimitri.

He looked down at the girl and bared his teeth. Then he climbed off the sofa and snatched the phone.

"Speak," he said into the receiver.

"He escaped the ambush," the voice said. It sounded far away.

"Well that is no bloody use to anybody, is it?"

"No, Scorpion."

"And the weapons?"

"Recovered, sir. We have them."

"This isn't sending a good message to the others who try

to steal our business, is it Chovka? You know we still have to kill the smuggler, don't you?"

"Yes sir, I will take care of it right away."

The Scorpion paused and looked at the girl. Tears ran down her face, she had her hand up to her nose and dabbed at the blood as it ran onto her hand.

A red speck hit the creamy-white sofa.

"I don't pay you to think, do I, Chovka?"

There was no reply.

"Don't just kill him like some dog in the street. We have him in a position now, a position where he is injured, limping. A position we control. We don't kill him, yet. We need everyone to know that we control the weapons in Africa. We crush any challenge, and we do not blink first."

The Scorpion went back to the sofa and sat down, he handed the girl a napkin without looking at her.

"It is the end game now Chovka. No. No. I have a plan. You see? There are more ways to kill a fox, we can also choke it with cream."

"I don't understand, Scorpion."

"That is okay. I do. Who supplied the guns?"

"That Greek bastard, Basil."

"I see. So, let's pay his debt off. We buy the debt from that dirty Greek crook, like our good friends the Rothschilds would. And then? He owes *us* the money for the guns, yes?"

"Yes."

"So let him pay. And, if he can't, we will get him to do something for us. Maybe, instead of chasing this fox, we let him come to us. And he can bring with him a big bowl of cream."

He dabbed his forefinger in the blood on the sofa and tasted it on the tip of his tongue and hung up the phone.

Scorpion handed it back to the suit.

"Fetch me another girl, Dimitri. This one is going to have an accident."

Matadi, Democratic Republic of Congo

THE REBELS HAD FIRED WILDLY AS STIRLING RAN. HE'D disappeared into the bush, hard targeting as bursts of gunfire *zipped* and *snapped* and slammed into the leaves and branches around him. He'd moved fast to get out of the killing area.

Now, he marched through the night back to the border. It was careful work. He moved in bursts, from cover to cover, listening for the rebels who might have followed, or wild animals crouched in trees ready to pounce and sink their teeth into his neck.

He could see the Matadi suspension bridge in the dark. It was built by the Japanese and spanned the great Congo River. He hid out of sight, near the road and with the lights on top of the bridge in view. It was just before dawn and he kept a look out for VD's pick-up truck. The plan had been for Stirling to sell the weapons in Kinshasa for cash, detonate the plastic explosive to destroy the cache, and kill as many rebels as possible. That *was* the plan, but now he was in trouble and early to the rendezvous.

The border crossing was calm in the early morning. Africans liked to move in the light, like any people of a wild land. They had a right to fear the dark and there were enough legends and folklore demons and evil spirits to stop children running off in the night.

Stirling saw a vehicle pull up to the guard hut and watched

it closely. He saw the Afrikaner resting his forearm on the door and sharing a joke with the overnight sentry. He was relieved, in spite of the pain in his stomach, he hadn't eaten since dishing out sweets to the kids on the previous morning.

The pick-up trundled down the dirt track towards him. It squeaked and jolted from side to side and Stirling saw VD in front with his bush hat on, singing along to some kind of South African country music. His name was Johan van Driebek, but Stirling called him VD for short. A sort of inside joke that Johan wasn't party to. They'd met in Luanda doing private security work together. VD was an old hand at the mercenary game in Africa and took Stirling under his wing.

Stirling stepped out from his hiding place and in front of the left headlight. VD braked hard and swerved and covered Stirling and the pick-up in a coat of dust.

"*Fokken hell, bliksem*," VD hollered and swore in Afrikaans out the window. "What the hell are you doing here, this isn't where we are supposed to – " his rant tailed off while Stirling walked around and got in. The rusted door scraped and whined as he pulled it shut. They were both large men and the cab was cramped.

"Hell, good to see you too, partner," Stirling said and they shook hands and Stirling grinned as VD calmed down.

"Please get me the out of here. It's been one hell of a night," he said.

VD was wide and round and used his Popeye-style forearms to turn the pick-up around. He bumped over the grass verge and overcorrected to get it back on track and back towards the border. They waved as they drove back into Angola and the guards watched curiously as they trundled back across the bridge.

"What's that?" VD said looking at the battered pink box on Stirling's lap.

"Semtex," Stirling said. "So drive carefully, hey?"

VD kept a straight face and pretended to concentrate on the road.

"Plastic explosive in pink wrapping paper? Cute," he said. "So what the hell happened? I told you not to go into the Congo alone, didn't I?" he shook his head, making it clear he was feeling a bit sniffy. "So?"

"You were right, kind of," Stirling said.

"Kind of? I told you not to do any gun deals. The Chechens own that action. I said they would try and kill you. Didn't I?"

"You did."

VD massaged his reddish beard.

"So what happened?" he asked.

"I was hijacked."

VD looked at him open-mouthed and then his eyes narrowed disbelievingly.

"Watch the road please," Stirling said and jostled the wheel to keep them on the track. The pick-up lurched and VD turned the wheel to keep them steady.

"No one is dumb enough to rip off that shipment," VD said and regained control.

"That's what I thought too. But I don't think they were only after the guns. They were trying to send a message."

"What message?"

"Don't screw with us," Stirling said flatly.

"So, what then? You think they wanted you?"

"I know they did."

"How?"

"The lead guy had empty vials on him. To fill up with fifty-cc of me. My blood as proof of death."

"Shitting hell, shitting hell. I told you! I told you! Don't mess with those guys man."

"Listen, VD," Stirling said. "I wasn't *just* going into the Congo to sell weapons to those rebels."

"Huh? What you mean?" VD watched him out the corner of his eye. Stirling knew he couldn't tell VD the truth, but he didn't want to lie to his friend either.

"I needed to rock the boat. Kick the hornets' nest. I needed to see if I could find the buyers, and you know … "

"What? No I don't know. What you mean, take them out?"

Stirling nodded. "Yup."

"What! Why? Are you *stupid*?"

"No, listen." Stirling waited to make sure VD was doing that.

"Okay. I should have told you sooner. Brought you up to speed."

"Finally. Something I agree with," VD nodded.

"These guys, selling weapons, they are very bad men. Those weapons kill civilians, children, they chop off their arms. Selling them to the same people who massacred people in Rwanda, and is anyone doing anything about it?"

"No," VD said, "so what, you were going to make these guys have an accident?"

"Eventually, after I found out who the players were and worked my way up to the big boys. Undercut the Chechens and then cut off the demand," Stirling locked eyes with VD. "Watch the bloody road," Stirling said.

VD laughed.

"Okay, so why?" he asked.

"Look, when I was in theatre I lost guys. Boys who trusted me and who I trusted with my life. And I lost those guys, cut down by illegal seven-six-two rounds from China and bomb-making kits from Iran."

"Afghan?"

"Yeah," Stirling nodded. "So I can't do anything about that, right? They binned me. But I can try here."

"Ja, try something *bloody crazy*, man," VD said.

"I am going to put a stop to the weapons. Well, I was, until I got hijacked."

"And now?

"I don't know. I still owe the suppliers for the shipment, so there is that," Stirling said.

"Wait, that scaly Greek bastard sold you the guns on credit?" VD spat. "How much?"

"A lot, more than I can get by tomorrow – and the juice is running. I have a big debt now. I was going to sell them, blow them up, and pay the Greek."

VD whistled. "You must be able to sell ice to an Eskimo if you convinced those guys to give you guns on credit," VD shook his head. "They're going to kill you, man."

They sat in silence and the headlights swished along in the darkness. VD started tapping the steering wheel and turned the music up and it hissed louder.

"I think I have an idea," VD said. "We can't get it all, but maybe we can get some, and get that Greek slime-ball to lay off you for a while. What do you reckon?"

"I'm all ears."

"How about you meet me at the nightclub tonight?"

"Which nightclub?"

"Buala Blues."

Stirling laughed. "What the hell you want to go there for?"

VD nodded along to the beat and watched the Angolan bush glide past at a calm forty miles per hour. Stirling watched him out the corner of his eye. *What was this Dutchman up to?*

CHAPTER THREE

They drove all day and around dusk made their way past the red-tiled roofs of the old colonial buildings along the beach front in Luanda. Stirling felt safer and looked out of the beaten up pick-up at the port city. It was split between new and old, wealthy and poor. Modern glass skyscrapers, opposite clay-tiled roofs of the historic Portuguese quarter. The derelict shanties of informal settlements and their destitute owners lapped at the city like the tide.

After dark, VD led Stirling walking through the shanty town. Dogs barked as they made their way down the narrow passages between densely packed dwellings. VD took Stirling down a green passageway and a tube of light flickered on the ceiling. VD paid a bouncer and he banged rapidly on a steel door. He ushered VD inside and Stirling stepped through the doorway.

"What're we doing here?" Stirling asked over the music.

They stood in the crowded nightclub, and past VD there was a tired looking boxing ring and stained mat, squared off with decking rope. VD looked around as if he hadn't heard; the music was loud and the nightclub was filled wall-to-wall with dancing people. Over on the stage a band of three horns and a drummer played while a woman in colourful dress danced and sang. The antique boxing ring was in front of the band.

Yellow electric lightbulbs hung from beams along the warehouse roof, wrapped in red acetate sheeting which gave the place a pink-grapefruit glow. The people jived and shouted and drank spirits out of clear plastic cups. They were the only white faces in the place. Stirling watched VD's mouth and tried to hear. It opened and closed and he waved his hands, but Stirling shook his head and couldn't make out what he was saying. Stirling pointed to his ear and shook his head. VD leaned in and pulled Stirling's shoulder to his chin.

"*Ag*, go get a drink and relax man. Look who is at the bar, you know him," he said and pointed at the bar, "I need to talk to somebody."

To continue reading on kindle, please press: https://geni.us/1BloodFeud

---

End of excerpt. © Reprinted by permission. All rights reserved.

JOIN THE HUNTING PARTY

Would you like a FREE top-secret psychological profile AND a Stirling Hunt Mission short story sent straight to your favourite device?

Just tell me where to send it at: www.stewartclydeauthor.com.

I try to publish new books often. I wake up, walk the dog, drink coffee, write novels, eat, sleep, repeat. If you'd like a notification when a new book hits the shelves, sign up and I'll send you a quick heads up with a direct link when a new one is released. That's all, nothing more, nothing less.

The events in DANGEROUS CARGO directly precede the book #1 in the Stirling Hunt Mission series, ENGLISH ASSASSIN.

Visit www.stewartclydeauthor.com to sign up and read it now.

A REVIEW REQUEST

You've come to the end of English Assassin. I hope you've enjoyed the series so far!

If you have, you'd make this author very happy if you would please click here to leave the book **a positive review**.

So many people are involved in publishing a book, but none are as important as you. If you enjoyed the story and have five minutes, I would be very grateful.

Please leave your review by **pressing here now**.

Thank you in advance!

Best,

Stewart Clyde

ALSO BY STEWART CLYDE

Never fear, the action continues in Blood Feud with one man's quest to bring a terrorist to justice.

Have you read them all?

Press on the title to learn more:

[Blood Feud](#)

[Black Beach](#)

[Red Vendetta](#)

ABOUT THE AUTHOR

Stewart Clyde is a new voice in the thriller genre. He is an Amazon charts best selling author and former British Army officer.

He has a degree in Politics & International Relations. After graduation, he moved to London and joined the army.

He's lived in eight countries, including the United States and Germany, and travelled to over forty. After almost a decade in the Armed Forces, he resigned his commission to write stories.

He likes riding motorcycles through the wine routes of the Iberian Peninsula and the Western Cape, but what he enjoys most is hearing from his readers. Please get in touch by visiting his website, or on social media.

For more please visit:
www.stewartclydeauthor.com

Join Stewart Clyde's social media
by pressing the button below

Printed in Great Britain
by Amazon